# Lunar Patrol

*Hunter Squadron*

David Hiers

This book is dedicated to my Mother, who badgered me into writing it after reading the short story, Lunar Rescue, as she wanted to know what happened next.

# CONTENTS

# PROLOGUE

Ephanorin approached the star gate, her Delorian star jumper in full stealth mode as was her custom. It paid to be stealthy in an often hostile universe. She was returning to the Sol system, which her people now called home after their birth-world had been destroyed by invaders. One last jump through the Jupiter Gate and she would be reunited with her pod mate, Talineer.

Passive sensors alerted her to several anomalies. Seconds later a strong sensor pulse emanated from near the gate. Despite her stealth settings, the pulse exposed her ship along with everything else in the vicinity.

She gasped. An entire armada of warships was massed at the stargate. They could have only one destination — Sol system. Fighters appeared all around her and her shields flared with multiple hits. In an instant, she spun her ship around and kicked the engines on full. Her ship was designed to scout, not fight. It excelled at two things, stealth and speed. Stealth was gone. She would have to rely on speed.

She quickly passed out of the fighters' range. She had to warn her people of the impending attack. Scanning the sector, she realized she could not get through her intended gate. Even with her speed, there were too many warships nearby. She would have to get to Sol system another way. There was another gate in this system. Little used as it passed through a backwater system, but in a roundabout way she could make it home.

Sensors showed the other gate was clear, it was of no interest to the armada. Her onboard A.I. calculated that the closest pursuers would not be able to catch her before she reached the gate. Thank the universe for speed, she thought. She was seconds from the gate when the stars shimmered. A huge ship materialized between her and the gate, firing even as it appeared.

A destroyer, she realized as her screens flared with multiple hits.

Then everything went dark.

# CHAPTER ONE

Liam was swimming laps in West Florida University's pool early in the morning, his mind wandering as he swam his mile. He did not have to report for flight training until 10:00 that morning, so he had plenty of time. A First Lieutenant with the United States Coast Guard, he had been picked to transition to aircraft and had almost completed his basic flight training on T-6B Texans at Whiting Field, near Pensacola, Florida.

IIe had hoped his next step would be to the Coast Guard's HU-25 Guardian, their medium range surveillance jet. But now that the Coast Guard was phasing them out, it looked like the Ocean Sentry would be his best option. A turbo prop aircraft, it was a lot slower than the Guardian, but it would still allow him to fly, while performing rescue or drug interdiction missions. Not a bad life for a 26-year-old from East Hartford, Connecticut. The goal for most of his High School classmates had been to work for Pratt & Whitney. He had made it out.

So far, he had been very happy with his life in the Coast Guard. He had six years in to date and planned to do his twenty, particularly now that they had chosen him for flight training. He was satisfied. Or had been until two months ago.

Two months ago, he discovered a whole new world. One he had never imagined. For a brief twelve hours, he had been part of that amazing world. He had flown to the Moon to conduct a rescue, barely making it back alive after being attacked by an alien fighter. Back on Earth, no one knew about his adventure. No one would believe him if he told them because aliens did not exist and space travel was in its infancy — mankind had not been to the moon since 1972. When he told his roommate, he had almost been sent for a psyche exam. So now he was back in flight training, knowing that space flight was possible and that he had no way to ever do it again.

Paul, the mysterious man who had taken him to the Moon, had disappeared and Liam had no idea how to contact him. How could he be satisfied now that he knew so much more was out there? He had to struggle to pay attention as even flight training seemed dull in comparison. At night he would stare at the stars, knowing there were aliens just out of sight and wondering how much more was out there. It was like being trapped in East Hartford again, with no hope of getting out. But hard work had allowed him to escape East

Hartford. There was nothing he could do to find that hidden world.

"Mind if I share the lane with you?" A voice interrupted his thoughts as he neared the end of the pool.

Liam stopped and looked up. Standing on the pool deck holding a kickboard and a pair of fins was a tall black man, bald headed with a very short white beard. "Paul, where have you been? I haven't seen you in two months. I don't even have your phone number. Do you know how much trouble I got into?" The questions rushed out as Liam stood in chest deep water.

"Nice to see you too," Paul replied as he slid into the pool next to Liam. "I had a set back with my shoulder injury, so I had to skip swimming for a while. But now I have been cleared, so I can swim again."

Liam just stared. "That's it? After we...," Liam hesitated, glancing around at the other swimmers. He did not want to say 'traveled to the Moon' in public. "After what we went through?" he finally said. "I thought I would never see you again? It's been months."

"I did wave at you a week later," Paul said as he adjusted his swim goggles.

"Yea," Liam laughed, thinking back to that day that Paul briefly uncloaked his alien fighter while Liam was flying. "I almost crashed when I saw you and then missed my next turn."

"I noticed," Paul said. "I almost told you about the turn, but I thought that if I spoke to you on the radio, you might freak out."

"That's a true statement."

"I have to get my swim in," Paul said. "But I would like to talk to you, so don't leave without saying goodbye first. Ok?"

"Uh, Sure," Liam muttered, a million questions on his mind. Paul kicked off the wall and started swimming his laps as Liam stared after him. This was so weird, Liam thought. Two months ago, he and Paul had rescued an alien on the Moon and had almost been shot down in the process. Then Paul disappears and when he shows up again, he acts like nothing out the ordinary occurred. Yet it had turned Liam's life upside down, or at least his perspective. Nothing seemed the same anymore.

Liam watched Paul swim the length of the pool, flip at the end and swim back. When Paul flipped again and started swimming away, Liam realized there would be no talking with him until he finished his laps. So, Liam started swimming again, his mind trying to prioritize the million questions he had for Paul when he finally finished swimming.

The swim lasted forever. It was not that it really took that long, only thirty minutes or so. It was the anticipation of finally getting some answers that made it seem to take forever. In the locker room and then the walk to the parking lot, Paul would not talk about anything more substantive than the weather. As they approached the parking lot, Liam spotted Paul's pale gold Honda Accord. It looked like any Honda Accord, but Liam knew that was merely camouflage. The Honda was actually the shuttle that had flown Paul and Liam to the Moon during the rescue mission. It had an alien A.I. operating system named Al and technology that allowed it to change its appearance.

Paul opened the driver's door. "I don't have much time. Got to get to work. But hop in for a second."

"The last time I got in your car I ended up on the Moon," Liam said.

"That's a fanciful way of putting it," Paul said with a laugh.

Liam looked at Paul quizzically. What did he mean by that? That is exactly what happened last time.

"Hop in," Paul repeated.

Liam climbed in the passenger side. The minute he closed the door Paul said, "We don't talk about those things in the open. Just in case someone is listening. They can't hear us in here, the shuttle blocks eavesdropping."

"Oh, good," Liam stuttered. "Because for a second there, I thought I was going crazy. That I imagined it or something."

Paul laughed. "Easy to do in this business. It's like living in an alternate world that only you can see."

"Exactly," Liam agreed, thinking back to the last two months. "Everything around you looks normal, but you know it's not."

"It takes a while to get used to it," Paul agreed. "Anyway, I was wondering if you would like to take another trip?"

Liam's heart jumped. He had been dreaming about getting back to this world. Flying in space. Meeting aliens. Discovering what was really out there. How could he possibly say no to that? Rather than saying any of that, Liam managed to ask, "Does it involve getting shot at?"

"Hopefully not," Paul said with a laugh. "You have been invited back to the island. Sally wants to thank you for helping her."

"Sally?"

"That's the name I use for our passenger. The one you rescued from the escape pod. I can't pronounce her real name. She has fully recovered and would like to thank you personally for saving her."

"Sure," Liam said quickly, his mind vividly replaying the rescue. Walking across the surface of the Moon, his feet leaving footprints in two inches of gray Moon dirt. Digging out the access port on the crashed escape pod. Carrying the smaller pod to the shuttle, while watching his oxygen supply dwindle. Being shot at by an alien fighter while returning to Earth. Meeting a group of aliens when they landed at a secluded island somewhere in the Pacific. Vivid memories of an impossible adventure.

"What?" Liam asked when he realized that Paul had been talking to him.

"I was thinking tonight," Paul repeated. "I could pick you up after you get off work and then get you back early in the morning. You probably should pack your flight clothes in case we take too long."

"No side trip to the Moon?" Liam tried to ask lightheartedly, thrilled that he was about to enter that alien world again.

"No. Just a very boring meet and greet."

"Sally is an alien, right?" Liam asked.

"Yes. So just a very boring meet and greet with an alien," Paul corrected.

"I'm in," Liam said enthusiastically. "You don't know how hard it has been the last two months. Knowing what is out there and also knowing there is no way I can do anything about it, to contact it. I didn't even know how to contact you. It was maddening."

"Sorry about that," Paul said. "Things got a little complicated and I got sidetracked. I will try to make it up to you."

"Just don't disappear again. Now that I know what is out there, I want to be part of it."

"Be careful what you wish for," Paul responded.

# CHAPTER TWO

The rest of the day crawled by. Liam even had trouble concentrating on his training flight, earning him a rebuke from his instructor. But how could he concentrate on flying a prop plane when he would fly in a space shuttle after work? Somehow, he managed to pass the flight and get through the day. He was sitting on his front porch, packed flight bag sitting next to him, when Paul's gold Honda finally turned down his street. Liam ran out and met Paul before he could pull into the driveway.

"You ready?" Paul asked as Liam jumped into the passenger seat, stowed his bag at his feet and closed the door.

"Yes," Liam said, failing to keep the excitement out of his voice.

Liam noticed that Paul was wearing his sun glasses, although the sun had already set. He remembered those glasses were an optical interface with the shuttle, providing Paul with much more 'sight' than the night vision goggles that Liam sometimes wore during flight training. Paul drove off, turning down a dark side street. Suddenly, they were in the air.

"I don't think I will ever get used to that," Liam said, as he looked down at the lights of the town receding below them. "I never felt you lift off."

"It is neat," Paul agreed. "They fixed the inertial dampeners since you were in here last."

"You mean since we were shot by that fighter?"

"Yes, then," Paul said.

When Liam tore his eyes off the view outside, he noticed that the passenger compartment had morphed. He was no longer in a Honda, he was in a space shuttle. "How does it do that again?" Liam asked, pointing to the dashboard that was no longer a dashboard, but a flat control panel.

"I have no idea," Paul admitted. "To me, it's magic. The Delorians tried to explain it to me one time, but the translation sounded something like molecular reassignment. I just know it can do it. You need to put on the space suit again. The one under the seat."

"We're going into space?"

"Low orbit, yes. But it is really for when we arrive. Avoids contamination."

Liam reached under the seat and pulled out the packet that contained the space suit. He pulled the thin membrane that was the space suit out and laid it on the front dash. "I still say this thing looks like a dive skin. There really is nothing to it," he said as he rubbed the thin material between his fingers."

"I could ask NASA to loan me one of their big bulky suits if you prefer," Paul said. "But I don't know how you would put it on in here."

"It's not easy putting on this one in here," Liam said as squirmed around, trying to peel off his clothes. "You really need to come up with a better way of getting into these spacesuits than doing these contortions in the front seat of your car," he complained. Liam finally managed to take his clothes off and stuffed them into the bag and sealed it. Then he started the contortions all over as he tried to slide his legs into the legs of the spacesuit and then pull the suit over his butt while getting his arms in. Feeling ridiculous as he fought with the suit in the confines of his seat, he glanced over to see Paul watching him with a bemused smile on his face.

"What?" Liam asked.

"If we weren't parked here at 10,000 feet waiting for you to get dressed, we could be halfway to the moon right now," Paul chuckled. "It really is not that difficult."

"How come I don't see you changing?" Liam asked, realizing that Paul was still wearing his pants and a long sleeve shirt.

"I have my suit on under my clothes," Paul responded. "I changed at home. You don't think I'm going to try to change in here, do you?"

Liam bit back his rhetorical comment and concentrated on putting on his suit. "Do I need to put on the face mask?" Liam asked as he finally pulled the suit up over his shoulders and sealed it.

"No. Not yet. Now store your civvies and your flight bag in the back so they don't float around during the flight."

Liam twisted around in his seat and stored both bags in the back seat with what looked like a Velcro mat. Then he flopped back into his seat.

"Belt up," Paul said.

"I thought you said the inertial dampener thingies were fixed," Liam said as he reached for the seat restraints.

"They are," Paul said. "The restraints are for if they fail."

"That's a comforting thought," Liam said as he snapped the belts in place. No sooner had he finished, than the shuttle leaped into the sky. The night became blacker and the stars clearer. To the west he could see the terminator line where the sun had not yet set over the Earth. As they moved higher, he could see the line where the Earth's blue-tinged atmosphere ended and the black of space began. His eyes registered the movement, but it felt like he was sitting still. "Those dampener thingies work well," Liam said. "How many g's did we just do?"

"More than you would have liked, I can assure you," Paul said.

Liam stared out the window - viewport - he corrected himself, as the Earth slowly rotated beneath him. He wanted this with all his being. He glanced back inside at the control console. The instrumentation was unrecognizable. Numbers flowed across some screens while others contained icons representing who knew what. Others had wavy lines with different color codes or starburst patterns. It reminded him of the first time he got into an aircraft cockpit and wondered what all the instruments meant. Now learning them seemed child's play compared to the shuttle's controls.

"Are you flying this, or is the A.I.?" Liam asked.

"I am," Paul answered. "I could let Al fly it, but what is the fun in that? I do let him drive when it is a Honda though. Makes a Tesla look like a Model T. And I get to take a nap or work on something else. But flying, no, I do that."

"How did you learn to understand all this?" Liam asked, motioning to the screens. "I don't understand any of it."

"It's confusing at first, like anything," Paul agreed. "Probably like when you first learned how to fly. But like flying, you learn it. The Delorians have a virtual reality type program which makes it quicker to understand. You still have to train and practice, but it speeds up the learning curve."

"Do you think they would let me train?" Liam asked quickly, unconsciously holding his breath as he waited for the response.

Paul glanced over at Liam. "You want to?"

"Are you kidding? Fly a space ship?" Liam gasped. "Yes! For the past two months all I could think about is what is out here and how could I get back to being a part of it. Like you said, the adventure of a lifetime. I just want the adventure to continue. I'm not ready for it to be over," Liam was a little embarrassed by his enthusiasm, but it was all true. His life had changed two months ago and he could not imagine going back. Not now. Not with what he had seen and done.

"I'll see what I can do," Paul said after considering for a minute. "It would be nice to have some company, someone I could talk to about what I am doing."

"Are you the only human working with the Delorians?" Liam asked surprised.

"No. But there are only a few and the others are not in the U.S. We don't get together very often. It is a bit lonely not being able to talk to anyone about what is going on."

Liam was quiet for the rest of the flight,

torn between thinking about the possibility of joining Paul and in awe of the view as the shuttle descended back into Earth's atmosphere. This time the trip was smooth. Liam considered commenting on how smooth the reentry was with no one shooting at them and the inertial dampeners working, but he was afraid to say it for fear it would jinx them so he waited till they landed to comment.

They flew through the upper atmosphere and into the clouds. When they emerged the blue of the Pacific Ocean filled Liam's view as far as he could see. They leveled off at five-hundred feet and screamed across the ocean. Liam was about to comment about the sonic boom they must be making, but held off as he realized that Paul was flying manually, not the A.I. and he did not want to distract him. Paul banked the craft back and forth as he dodged islands, a broad smile across his face. This was flying, Liam thought. I have got to do this.

Paul slowed over an island and quickly descended into a clearing, the same clearing they had landed in two months prior. The struts touched down gently.

"Seal your faceplate," Paul instructed.

As soon as Liam sealed his suit, the doors of the shuttle retracted into the roof.

"The seatbelt sign has been turned off and it is now safe to deplane the craft. Thank you for flying Delorian Space Lanes," Paul said with mock seriousness as he unbelted and climbed out of the shuttle.

Liam looked out at the clearing. It looked much like it had the last time he landed here. A grassy clearing about thirty yards wide, surrounded by jungle. As Liam climbed out of the shuttle, he looked down and spotted old burn marks on the vegetation from their landing two months ago. He looked back up, spying the path the Delorians had taken through the jungle. No one was there.

"Where is everyone?" Liam asked as he looked back to Paul.

"They are waiting for us," Paul answered as he headed across the clearing towards the path in the jungle. He was still wearing his "civvies" over his space suit and had not put up his hood.

"How come you are not wearing your hood?" Liam asked as he hurried to catch up with Paul.

"I don't have a contamination risk," Paul said.

"And I do?" Liam asked. "What do they have to worry about from me that you don't have?"

Paul laughed as he entered the jungle. "They are not worried about what you have. They have been on Earth for centuries. They are immune from Earth viruses. It's what you have to worry about catching from them."

Liam felt a chill run down his spine that belied the 90-degree temperature on the island. "What do I have to worry about?" he asked as he hurried to keep up with Paul. The sunlight filtered through the jungle canopy, playing tricks on his eyes as shadows danced across the path.

"Your system would not react well to alien viruses. That is why you are in your suit," Paul explained.

"How come you're not?"

"Because I have been vaccinated against them. I am immune. But you are not." The conversation ended as Paul stepped between two large palm trees and disappeared. Liam stepped between the trees and froze. In front of him was blackness. Not a shadow from the trees, just a black void. Behind him he could hear the jungle sounds and could feel a light breeze on his back, but in front of him was nothing.

"Paul?" Liam called out. "Paul, where are you?"

A disembodied hand reached out from the void. Liam screamed and jumped back, hitting his side against one of the trees. Before he could regain his balance, the hand grabbed him. Liam slapped at the hand as he was dragged into the void.

Liam stumbled into the void, still trying to get the hand off him. Another hand grabbed him by the shoulder. "Liam, Liam. Relax."

The voice finally registered. Paul was standing in front of him, holding him by the shoulders. It was dark, but no longer black. Liam's heart was pounding in his throat. "What the h... Don't you ever ... What were you..." Liam could not seem to finish a sentence. He took a step back, hitting a hard surface. He turned quickly. The door, or whatever it was, was gone. He was in a small cave, a little taller than him and about six feet wide. Behind Paul the cave extended a few more yards before it turned. There was just enough light to see.

"Take a deep breath," Paul was saying as he continued to hold Liam.

"Don't ever do that to me again," Liam finally managed to say. "That was the scariest thing I have ever seen."

"This from the man who performed a rescue on the moon and was shot at by a fighter on the way back?" Paul asked with a muffled chuckle. "You have an odd fright level."

Liam ignored the comment and just concentrated on getting his pulse and breathing back under control. After several deep breaths, he straightened up. "Any more surprises," he asked harshly.

"I don't know," Paul responded seriously. "I did not realize that your suit optics would not penetrate the door. I'm assuming that is what happened, you could not see past the entrance?"

"It was just a void, and then this hand reached out and grabbed me and pulled me inside."

"Yes. I'm glad I was wearing my suit. I think you would have broken my arm the way you were hitting me like that," Paul said. "But I had to pull you in quickly because the door only stays open a short while and you could not hear me because the entrance deadens all sound."

"What kind of door was that?" Liam asked, looking around. "And where is it now?"

"My answer to that and my answer to most of your questions once we go on is, 'I don't know.' I have no idea how any of this works any more than a caveman would understand electricity. I just tell myself it is alien tech and go with it. I recommend you do the same thing. Don't try to understand or make sense of anything at first. It will just confuse you more. Just go with it and then try to figure it out later if you feel you must. Can you do that?" Paul asked.

Liam considered for a moment. "Sure, I guess so. But is there anything else scary?"

"I don't think so," Paul said. "You have seen the Delorians already. They are alien, but not scary. And they are friendly, although their mannerisms may seem odd."

"Okay," Liam finally said. "Lead on."

Paul walked deeper into the cave with Liam at his heels. The passageway turned and they walked another twenty-five feet before Paul stopped in front a large hole in the floor about ten feet in diameter. "All right," Paul said. "This part might be a bit scary." Liam waited. "This is an elevator," Paul finished.

"How do we call it up?" Liam asked when he saw no obvious controls.

"That's the scary part," Paul said. "There is no elevator car. The shaft here is the elevator. You just step into it and it takes you down."

Liam looked over the edge of the lip. He could not see the bottom in the dim light. "How fast does it take you down?" Liam asked, imagining falling hundreds of feet.

"Pretty fast," Paul admitted. "But the landing is smooth. You want me to go first or do you want to go together?"

"I'm not letting you out of my sight again," Liam said, still shook up from earlier.

"Okay," Paul said. "Hold my hand and we will step out together. Actually, we will leap because we want to go down the center of this shaft, not slide down the sides." Liam stood next to Paul and reached out to hold his hand. "On three, we will just hop out to the center there. Okay?" Liam nodded. "One, two, three…"

They leaped into the center of the space. Liam was not sure what to expect. He did not expect the lack of any sense of movement. No feeling of falling, no vertigo. But the wall whipped past as if he were falling. Almost like watching a movie from the safety of your chair. And then it was over. They were standing on a platform overlooking a large subterranean cavern brightly lit from above, but from no obvious lighting source. The cavern was filled from floor to ceiling with at least a hundred Delorian space ships, that appeared to be just floating.

Liam stared. "They are beautiful," he whispered in awe. Indeed, they were the most elegant craft he had ever seen. They appeared to be about the same size as an F-18 Hornet, which Liam remembered from flight school was 56' long, 37' 5" from wingtip to wingtip, and 15' 3.5" high. But there the similarity ended. The fuselage of the Delorian craft was much wider than the F-18, making it look like two pilots could sit side by side, rather than fore and aft.

The fuselage expanded as it went back, forming almost a triangle, although everything on this craft had elegant flowing lines. There did not appear to be a sharp edge anywhere. And then there were the wings, or whatever they were since they probably could not act as a wing in atmosphere. There were four of them, two on the top and two on the bottom. The top two seemed to flow out of the back of the craft, angled up about 30 degrees and then flowed forward along the side of the craft, tapering off until they ended in rounded points near the front where the cockpit should be. Another set of wings came out the bottom and mirrored the top set. Between the upper and lower wing, near the base were two large pods, one on each side. The entire craft was a deep, dark blue that was almost black.

"The Delorians create very elegant craft," Paul agreed. "Nothing ugly like that fighter that attacked us."

"These are fighters," Liam said, rather than asked. Although they were gorgeous, the design cried out fighter.

"Yes. They are Delorian fighters."

Liam stared at the craft, trying to figure out how many there were floating in this cavern and trying to figure out why they looked vaguely familiar. And then he had it. "Those are X-wing fighters!" he exclaimed. "Oh my God, those are X-wings!"

Paul looked at him and snorted. "You watch way too many movies."

"No. Look at them. They are X-wings," Liam insisted.

Paul looked at the ships and then back at Liam. "Okay. They do have four pilons or wings on them, I will grant you that. But otherwise, they are nothing like an X-wing. These are much more elegant and the dimensions are all wrong."

"They are X-wings, the next generation," Liam insisted.

"Do you do anything other than watch movies?" Paul laughed.

"What are they doing here," Liam asked.

"Let's hope you never find out," Paul answered as he led Liam off the platform to a side opening in the cavern, while Liam kept staring back at the suspended fighters. "Remember, you are here to meet Sally."

They walked down a circular passageway that appeared to have been bored through rock as the walls, ceiling and floor were smooth, almost polished. Diffuse light glowed from the top of the passage, but again from no discernable source. Paul led them through an open door and then stopped. Liam looked around. They were in an oval shaped room, perhaps thirty or forty feet in diameter. Along the wall was a shelf at chest height that extended about two feet out. Multiple stools that looked a little too tall to be comfortable ranged along the wall. The ceiling was about twelve or fourteen feet high and was lit like the hallway.

"Not much into color schemes, are they?" Liam said as he noticed that the room, like the hallway, was a flat gray.

"I'm not sure they see color the same way we do," Paul said, as he walked over to a small metal box sitting on the shelf. He opened the lid and looked inside. Liam looked over his shoulder.

Inside was a small patch about the size of a silver dollar.

"What is that?" Liam asked. "It's a vaccine," Paul replied. "It immunizes you from the viruses the Delorians carry."

"You want me to take the vaccine," Liam asked skeptically.

"No," Paul said. "The question is whether you want to take it or not."

Liam looked at Paul quizzically. "Here's the deal," Paul explained. "You don't have to take it. But if you don't, you can't take off your suit around the Delorians. It is too dangerous for you. And that is fine. We will do the meet and greet with your suit on. If you take the vaccine, then you can take your helmet off and you don't have to be suited up every time you come here. I have taken the vaccine. It does not hurt. No side effects. The choice is yours."

"And I can come here again," Liam asked.

"They would not be offering it if they did not expect you to come back."

"No side effects?"

"None."

"Sign me up," Liam said with no further hesitation.

"Unseal your facemask and slide off your hood," Paul instructed. Liam did as requested and Paul took out the patch. "I'm going to place this on the side of your neck. It will feel warm for a second or two and that is it. Ready?"

"Go for it," Liam said.

"That's it?" Liam asked when the warmth died down a few seconds later.

"Yep, that's it. That wasn't so bad, was it?

Before Liam could respond, the far door opened and a Delorian walked in. Unlike the previous ones he had seen, this Delorian was not wearing a helmet. Liam could not help staring. The Delorian was easily a foot or two taller than him, with a tall, thin body. It was wearing a suit like Liam's 'dive skin' so it outlined the Delorians dimensions. The legs were long and thin and the knees bent backwards. The torso was thin, but the chest was large with three prominent, large, flat ribs that flared from the hips up to the shoulders. The arms were long and thin with an extra elbow that was unsettling. The head was not covered. The skin was a gray, with a slight iridescent blue dusting.

The head was roughly triangular, but with rounded edges. The chin was at the bottom of the triangle, with a horizontal slit that might be a mouth. The cheek bones were very prominent, running up the side of the head. The eyes were huge, large tear-drop shaped that almost met at the top of where a nose should be, but wasn't, and then angled up diagonally. They were a deep brown and probably four inches long. The eyes were protected by a large bony ridge that jutted out and down over the sides of the head like the beginnings of flat horns that never developed.

The Delorian turned as if on display, and Liam saw that the back of the head was bare and had three distinct spheres. The Delorians back was the same as its front, with three prominent rib like structures forming the upper back area and then the abdomen narrowing down to the hips. The Delorian turned back to face Liam and then waited, while Liam continued to stare.

"This is Sally," Paul said at last, breaking the silence.

"Can she understand us?" Liam asked in a hushed whisper.

"She can. But you can't understand her," Paul answered. "She would like to give you a communicator. It will allow her to talk directly to you."

"Sure," Liam said.

"Remember," Paul continued. "Delorians are aliens. Their tech is very different from ours. The communicator is a patch. She wants to attach it to your head right behind your ear."

"What?"

"You told me to warn you about things," Paul said. "It is really no big deal. I'm wearing one now. It attaches to your skin like a band aid. It is not invasive. You can take it off whenever you want.

But it will allow you to hear them. I just wanted you to know so you don't flip out when she walks over here and tries to put it on you. Are you good with this?"

"It's just a patch. It doesn't go inside me or anything," Liam asked nervously.

"That's right. It's like a conduction patch. If you don't want to..."

"No, no. It's okay. Tell her it is okay," Liam said.

"You just did," Paul answered.

Liam watched nervously as Sally walked slowly towards him. She held out her hand and showed him a circular patch the size of a dime. Liam looked at the patch and then stared at her hand. She had four gray, multi-jointed fingers that ended in round pads. She waited a moment longer and then slowly reached up to place it behind Liam's left ear. Liam froze, afraid to move and afraid not to. The touch was feather light. Then Sally stepped back to give Liam some space.

"Greetings, Earthling."

Liam jumped as the sound came from inside his head. He glanced at Paul, who was having trouble not laughing.

"Isn't that what aliens say in all the movies?" the voice in his head continued.

Now Paul was laughing. "The Delorians love that joke. They did the same thing with me years ago."

"Hello, Liam," the voice spoke again. "I am …" the next word was unpronounceable. "You can call me Sally. Paul says my actual name is too difficult for you."

"Hello, Sally," Liam said tentatively. "Nice to meet you." Liam felt foolish. He was meeting an alien for the first time, second time actually, and all he could say was 'nice to meet you.' What did you say to an alien?

"You have met me before, Liam. When you saved me on the Moon. I am very grateful. It was very brave of you to risk your life to save someone you did not know. It was very…" another unpronounceable word.

"Some words don't translate," Paul chimed in. You have to fill them in by context.

"You humans are an interesting race," Sally continued. "You have great capacity for kindness, and yet great capacity for evil, sometimes in the same individuals. If you survive the latter trait, you can be a great race."

"If," Liam heard Paul mutter beside him.

"We would like you to join us," Sally continued, "like Paul, as a liaison with your people."

Liam stood there dumbfounded. Then he realized that Sally was waiting for an answer.

"You will show yourself?" Liam asked.

"No. That would be catastrophic," Sally replied. "We no longer try to influence your development. We tried that thousands of years ago, but your species is too… complicated. We have decided to leave you be. Your race will live or die by your own hands, not ours. But we do need liaisons. Subtle approaches that only one human can do with another and we believe you have the necessary characteristics. If you are willing, we would like you to join Paul."

Liam could not believe what he was hearing. He was being invited into the world he had glimpsed and then thought he had lost forever.

"Yes. Yes," he stammered.

"Thank you," Sally said, before stepping over and hugging Liam. The embrace was awkward, almost like hugging a skeleton, but with a hint of great strength.

Sally stepped back.

"Good day, Liam," Sally said, before turning and walking out the door.

Liam stood there stunned, staring at the door Sally had just exited.

"Shall we go?" Paul asked.

"Go where? What just happened?" Liam asked confused.

"That was the boring meet and greet I warned you about," Paul said.

"I'm in? Am I in?" Liam asked.

"Come on," Paul said, taking him by the arm. "We need to go."

Liam allowed Paul to lead him out of the room and down the hall. His mind was reeling. What did this mean? What would he do? He stopped when they were back on the platform. "Will I get to fly one of those fighters?" Liam asked, staring out at the hundreds of fighters.

"Let's hope not," Paul answered seriously.

"What do you mean? Why not?" Liam asked, trying to imagine what it would be like to fly such a craft. And in space, no less.

"Because if you are flying a fighter, it means there are a bunch of enemy fighters trying to shoot you down. You already know what that feels like and it is not fun."

"Have you flown one of these," Liam asked, refusing to give up on this line of thought.

"These? Yes."

"When? What are they like?"

"I was the test pilot for them," Paul answered. "To see if humans could fly them."

"And?"

"And, yes they can be flown by humans. With modifications. And yes, they are real fun to fly, at least when people are not shooting at you," Paul said, as he led Liam back to the Delorian's version of an elevator. "Right now, I want to go topside. Since you are going to ask me a million questions, I might as well be resting in the tropical sun with my feet in the water when I answer them."

# CHAPTER THREE

Once back on the surface, Paul led Liam back to the shuttle. Paul reached into the back of the shuttle and pulled out two bathing suits. Tossing one to Liam, he said, "You can take off the space suit now. There is a small lagoon over there." He pointed off to the left. "Nice place to swim. I'll answer your questions there."

Liam stripped off the space suit and replaced it with the bathing suit and then followed Paul along another path that opened up to a small lagoon about one hundred feet in diameter. The blue water was crystal clear and colorful fish darted everywhere. The lagoon was bordered by the jungle on his side and by coral rocks on the other side. There was a small pebble beach that sloped gently into the water before it quickly dropped. The bottom appeared to be fifty or sixty feet below.

Paul walked across the beach into the water and then dove in. Liam followed, the cool water feeling good on his skin after wearing the space suit. Soon he was treading water next to Paul.

"As beautiful as this is," Liam said. "You have got to tell me more about the Delorians."

"Sure," Paul said. He swam back to the beach and sat down on the edge of the water, with Liam following closely behind. "What do you want to know?"

"Everything," Liam said. Then added, "Why was that meeting so short? Isn't there other stuff we need to talk about?"

Paul laughed. "I asked the same question the first time. The Delorians believe that first contact should be brief. They give you time to process that you have met an alien."

"I don't think I will ever get used to that," Liam admitted.

"It is pretty neat," Paul agreed. "Anyway. The Delorians keep the first meeting brief. After that will depend on what they want you to do. You will often go months without ever seeing them, and then out of the blue they will ask you to do something."

"Like what?"

"Most of the time it is explaining an event to them, from a human perspective. That is rather humbling as often you are explaining things that do not put humanity in the best light. Wars, terrorism, politics. Sometimes, they want to know how humans would use their technology. That can be fun, like learning to fly their fighters."

"Why do they have all those fighters here?" Liam asked. "Do you think they will take over Earth?"

Paul laughed. "You've been watching too many movies. No, I don't think they plan on taking over the Earth. They say they are here to protect us and I believe them. They have been here for centuries. If they wanted to take over, they could have done so long ago."

"So, why the fighters?" Liam asked again, thinking of the giant cavern below him filled with the fighters.

"It's hard to say. The Delorians are very... secretive, is probably the best word," Paul said. "What I have pieced together from my contact with them is that they believe minimal involvement with us is the best. I think they were known by the Aztecs and the ancient Egyptians and probably some others. But since then, they have stayed to themselves for the most part."

"Who are they protecting us from?"

"Other aliens is all I know," Paul said.

"And these other aliens are hostile?"

"All they tell me is there are a lot of aliens out there. Some are friendly, some are not. But I think there is more to it than that," Paul continued. "The Delorians believe that contact with any of the aliens, including them, would destroy our culture or our path. It would certainly radically change everything. They believe we should develop at our own pace. It's almost like a religion to them."

"So, why the fighters?" Liam asked again.

"I think that is for the hostile aliens."

"How many Delorians are there?" Liam asked.

"I don't know. I have seen up to fifteen here during my visits. I have heard reference to a couple of other places like this, but I have not been to them. I think one is in China and another in Australia. There may be more, I'm not sure. Their main base is near Jupiter. I have been there once. Quite impressive. The impression I have is that their population is small, hundreds or thousands, maybe. Not millions."

"You have been to Jupiter?"

"Yes."

"How cool is that? But where are they from? Where are the rest of them? Why are they protecting us? Why do they care?" Liam's questions were endless as he tried to understand this new world.

Paul held up his hands. "I don't know. If you find out, let me know. Like I said, they are pretty secretive. Something you will have to get used to."

"How? There is so much out there that we had no clue about. Don't you want to know all about it?"

"Sure, I do. But they will only tell you so much,

so I try to keep my eyes and ears open and piece together what I can. In the meantime, I enjoy experiencing what I can. Which is so much more than most people know about."

"That is true," Liam said, thinking about his trip to the moon. Liam sat in silence as he contemplated all that he had seen and heard. Paul had been right. This would be an adventure of a lifetime.

# CHAPTER FOUR

Stuck in rush hour traffic on a Friday afternoon in Mobile, Alabama, was not Liam's idea of fun. It had been two weeks since he had visited the Delorians and he had not seen or heard from Paul since. As the traffic slowly moved, his cell phone rang. There was no caller I.D. He let his car answer it, wondering if this was another scam call offering an extended car warranty. He had received six of those calls already this week.

"Liam, this is Paul," the caller identified himself when Liam answered. "Got any plans for tonight?"

Liam's heart skipped a beat. Every time Paul called something real interesting happened. "Uh, no. Not really. Why?" Liam stuttered. He remembered Paul had told him not to talk about the aliens and never, never, never mention them on the phone or internet as NSA would pick it up on their monitoring.

"I thought I would take the boat out. I need to do a check out trip, work out any bugs, and thought you might enjoy the trip. It should be fun," Paul replied.

Liam's mind raced. Was the boat the shuttle? Where was he planning on going? Were they going back in space? Or to visit the Delorians? Liam had plans to meet some of the other flight students for dinner and drinks, but he would gladly cancel those plans if it meant flying with Paul. "Uh, sure," Liam said. "Nothing I can't cancel. Do I need to bring anything special?"

"No. Everything you need I have on board," Paul replied.

That clinched it. Paul must mean the spacesuit in the shuttle. Liam could feel his heart racing in anticipation. Although it had only been two weeks since his 'meet and greet' with Sally, he had not seen Paul since and was starting to wonder when he would see him again. 26 years old, patience was not Liam's strong suit.

"Can I pick you up in about thirty minutes?" Paul asked.

Liam laughed. That was so Paul. Don't see him for weeks or months and then he wanted you right then. "Sure," Liam said. "I should be home by then, assuming this traffic does not get any worse."

"Ok, I'll see you then," and the call ended.

Liam had been patient with the traffic. But now all he wanted to do was get home. He begrudged every red light and cursed every car that slowed him down. He didn't worry about Paul getting to his house on time. With the shuttle, Paul could fly in stealth mode. Paul had explained that stealth mode had something to do with the skin of the shuttle bending light. The only thing Paul had to be concerned about was turning on stealth mode when someone was watching as the car would seem to just disappear. That would be awkward.

Liam arrived home with ten minutes to spare. He hurried inside and changed out of his flight suit and into a shirt and jeans and then went into the kitchen to grab something quick to eat. You never knew when you would get to eat around Paul. He was finishing a peanut butter and jelly sandwich when he saw Paul pull into his driveway. Liam downed a glass of milk, wiped his mouth with a kitchen towel and ran out the door.

His heart was racing by the time he climbed into Paul's 'Honda,' but it had nothing to do with his short sprint out the door. It was the anticipation of what would happen next. He glanced over at Paul and noticed that he had his space suit on under his clothes, the black fabric just visible under the V of his shirt. "Where are we going?" Liam asked as soon as he closed the door.

"Hello to you too," Paul said with a smile. "Not too excited, are we?" Paul did not wait for a response before continuing. "The Delorians have a satellite that has malfunctioned. They asked me to fix it. I could do it myself. It's not that hard. But it's like SCUBA diving. You can do it alone, but you really shouldn't. So, I wondered if you wanted to come along."

"Satellite? You mean a satellite in space?" Liam asked, realizing how stupid that question sounded.

"That's where satellites normally are," Paul answered. "And since you like me to spell everything out to you, I was wondering if you would like to do a spacewalk with me while I fix a satellite. In space," Paul added.

"A spacewalk? You are asking if I want to do a spacewalk?"

Paul backed out of the driveway and started driving down the street. "You really need to calm down," Paul said. "You would have thought I had invited you to..."

"... A frigging spacewalk!" Liam finished his sentence.

"Not quite the way I would have put it, but okay." Paul said. He drove down the street and then turned into a subdivision consisting of multiple townhouses.

"Where are you going?" Liam asked.

"I'm looking for a place to take off. Where we won't be noticed," Paul said as he pulled behind two townhouses where the dumpsters were located.

"It's still daylight, how are you going to take off without being noticed?"

"The shuttle does have a stealth mode," Paul said.

"I know, but you can't just disappear in front of someone."

Paul pulled around back and parked next to a dumpster. "Here's a good spot," he said.

"How do you know?" Liam asked. "Anyone could be looking out their windows at us right now."

"Actually, not," Paul said. "Al has tracked everyone around here by thermal scans and no one is near a back window. And he has jammed the camera over there so it never recorded us pulling around the back. Yep, this place is perfect."

"Al can track everything around us? That is... Whoa! You did it to me again," Liam said, as he watched the ground recede below him, but this time in the daylight. "And no one can see us, even though it is daytime?"

"That's right," Paul said. "Pretty neat technology." Paul stopped the shuttle at the thousand-foot mark. "Al, hold us at a hover here." He turned to Liam. "There is a lot of air traffic this time of day, so we will hold here while you change. You know where the space suit is. Time to put it on. And make sure your clothes are secured as we will open the doors when we get there. You don't want your clothes floating away. That would be kind of hard to explain," Paul finished with a laugh.

While they hovered, Paul pulled off his shirt and pants and stowed them. Liam once again had to struggle in the passenger seat while he first stripped down and then wiggled into the space suit. "You really need to get more adept at that. What if we were in a hurry?" Paul asked.

"Then you would let me change at home where I have more room than in the front seat," Liam responded.

By the time Liam was securing his clothes, the inside of the car had turned into a shuttle. "I can see there are a lot of things about this life I will never get used to," Liam said. "Like the way this car morphs back and forth into a shuttle."

"It is weird," Paul agreed. "Want to drive?"

"Fly the shuttle?" Liam asked. "Yes. But I don't have a clue what to do."

"The shuttle is easy," Paul explained. "Remember, it was modified to allow humans, specifically me, to operate it. The Delorians kept the steering wheel and the pedals. Gas is still gas. Brake is brake, although it really is reverse thrust. The steering wheel doesn't work like a car anymore, rather it works like a steering wheel on a plane. You can pull it out and push it back in and, of course, turn it."

"What about all the buttons on the wheel?"

Liam asked.

"They activate different menus on the panel here. This set is comm. This cluster is navigation. These control different sensor arrays. On the panel here," Paul indicated the console between the two seats, "you can choose different thrust options. One works in atmosphere, the other in space flight. There are also toggles here which activate certain functions, depending on what menu you are in. And of course, life support. The doors work with the same controls as they do when it is a car. All in all, pretty simple."

"Simple for you maybe," Liam said.

"Well, if you don't want to fly it, that's okay."

"No, I really do. I just don't know if I can," Liam said.

"It's okay, I'll keep you out of trouble," Paul said. "Al, configure the cockpit for dual controls."

Liam watched as the panel if front of him flowed until it mirrored Paul's side, complete with a steering wheel and pedals.

Paul walked Liam through the controls once again, stopping at navigation. "Now scroll through the navigation window," Paul instructed. "This is how you choose your destination. Select Satellite 974. Now choose the flight path on the display. See how your destination and the flight path are shown in your heads-up display?"

"Yes."

"It's just like a GPS in your car, or really more like on a boat. Here is your destination and this line is your optimal projected flight path. This other line is your actual path. So, all you have to do is to keep those two paths together."

"What are all the numbers on the side?" Liam asked.

"You can modify those anyway you want," Paul answered. "Right now the numbers by the satellite icon show the distance to target in miles and time to target based upon the projected path and also based upon the current progress. The current is blacked out now because we are not moving. You can set the target for actual location, like your latitude and longitude lines that you are familiar with, only in three dimensions, not two, and a myriad of other configurations."

"It says 347,305 miles," Liam said. "Is that right?"

"Yes," Paul answered. "The satellite we have to service is about 100,000 miles past the Moon."

"Past the Moon?" Liam said. "I am never going to get used to this."

"You do," Paul said. "But it will always be amazing."

"I bet," Liam agreed.

"If you are ready," Paul said. "Treat this like a plane and slowly follow the flight path on the heads-up display. Al will monitor other traffic so we don't run into anyone, like that Delta flight coming this way."

Liam pushed on the gas pedal and pulled back on the wheel. The shuttle banked and shot into the sky, the numbers on the heads-up display spinning.

"Easy does it," Paul said. "Not so hard. We have a lot of horses under this hood."

"Sorry," Liam said as he backed off and tried to settle his actual course line onto the projected path. After a few attempts he managed to center the line almost dead on.

"There," Paul said. "It's not that bad. See, you are a natural."

"It's not bad when you are walking me through it," Liam agreed.

Paul continued to coach Liam as they accelerated away from Earth. As the sky turned from blue to black, Paul said, "Okay, now you have to change drives. Activate the thrusters by pushing here on the center console. We are transitioning from atmospheric drive to what I call space drive. The Delorian word for it is impossible," Paul added apologetically.

"In space," Paul continued. "Your actions have to be very precise. You don't need a lot of force to move as there is no friction. But you also have to use reverse thrusters to slow down, again because there is no friction to slow you down once you are out of the gravity well."

Liam flew for an hour while Paul patiently coached him. He barely noticed the Earth shrinking behind him or the moon off to his right as he was fixated on the controls and the console. As they neared the target satellite, he thought he was starting to get the hang of it.

"Let me take it in from here," Paul said as they neared the broken satellite. "This will take a little finesse and I don't want you to have all the fun."

"You have the controls," Liam said, as he had been trained in flight school.

"I have the controls," Paul said. He deftly pulled the shuttle within twenty feet of the satellite and then spun the shuttle so it was between the Earth and the satellite with Liam's side door facing the satellite. Once Paul matched speed with the satellite he instructed Al to maintain the relative distance to the satellite and then turned to Liam to explain their mission.

"Here's the plan," Paul said. "Once we get suited up, I will open the side doors of the shuttle. You and I will both be tethered to the shuttle so you don't float away. That would ruin your whole day. You can't swim in space. You will have this wand," Paul said, holding up a twelve-inch-long rod that looked like a wand, but with a fat base. "It is very basic. It shoots $CO_2$, which will act as thrust and push you where you want to go. It does not hold very much, so use it sparingly."

"I will go and service the satellite. It probably just got fried by a solar flare. Once I figure out which component went bad, all I'll have to do is replace it. They are pretty simple to change out. You can just hang around. Stay near me, but don't touch me or the satellite as it will knock it off course and I will have to recalibrate it. Also, keep the shuttle between you and Earth. The shuttle is shielding us. We don't want anyone to see us. That would be awkward."

"How would they see us?" Liam asked. "We are 100,000 miles past the moon and are only a six-foot target."

"I know it seems unlikely," Paul agreed. "But we don't take risks. And there are thousands of telescopes looking this way at any given time. Some small and some really big. It would only take one sighting to potentially change the course of history."

"I suppose it would really freak someone out to see two people doing a space walk out past the moon."

"You think?" Paul said. "Any questions?"

"I just stay out of the way," Liam answered.

"That's the plan. Enjoy the view. This should be a cake walk."

"Ok. I think I can do that," Liam said.

"Pull up your hood and seal the faceplate," Paul instructed as he fastened a cuff on Liam's wrist. He then lowered the seats flat so there was more room in the shuttle.

"You could do that the whole time and you made me change in the seat?" Liam complained.

"We would have had to pull the seats back up before we flew," Paul answered. "Takes too much time." Paul showed Liam how to attach the harness to his suit and made sure that the tether was attached. "This is your lifeline," Paul said. "Without it you drift off into space. So pay attention to it." He then attached the wand on a short leash to Liam's harness, before making sure that his gear was set up. "Ok, you ready?" Paul asked when he was satisfied with the preparations.

"Ready," Liam said, his heart pounding. He glanced at the display on the upper right of his helmet, noting that the little man icon was green. Green is good, Liam repeated to himself.

"Hold on," Paul instructed. "I'm going to open the doors on your side. There will be some residual air loss that might push you."

Liam held on and the doors opened. He saw a slight puff of air turn into ice crystals and then stared out at the stars. Twenty feet away floated the Delorian satellite. It was the size of a small briefcase, with slender rings around it. It looked like a large diagram of an atom. Paul pushed off and floated out of the shuttle, heading for the satellite, his tether reeling out behind him. He stopped about a meter from the satellite and looked back at Liam. "Your turn," he said.

Liam tentatively pushed off and then panicked when he realized he was heading for Paul and would probably collide with him. He started flailing his arms and legs, but all that caused him to do was to start to rotate.

"Al, stop Liam's tether," Paul said.

Liam came to a sudden halt and started twisting at the end of the tether. "Sorry about that," he muttered."

"Don't worry," Paul said. "It's your first time in zero gravity. Use the wand to move around. But very short bursts until you get the hang of it. You don't want to jet around the shuttle like a tether ball. And make sure you don't run into my tether."

Paul watched while Liam experimented with the wand, moving slowly with short puffs of $CO_2$. Evidently satisfied Liam was okay, Paul used his own wand to slowly approach the satellite. "Let's have a look see," Liam heard Paul say to himself as he floated next to the satellite.

Liam slowly jetted away from the shuttle, trying to stay as far away from the satellite as he could while still keeping the shuttle between him and Earth. From his vantage point he had an unimpeded view of the moon, shining large in the

black of space. Liam could not believe his good
fortune. He was floating in space. He never even
dreamed about traveling in space. Life just did not
get any better than this.

"What is this?" Liam heard Paul asking himself.
A moment later, Paul said. "Oh no, they aren't
doing that to me again." The tone of his voice made
Liam glance over at Paul. He was pushing himself
away from the satellite, sending the satellite
spinning. "Liam," Paul yelled. "Get back to the
shuttle now. Al, retract Liam's tether, fast." Liam
was jerked by the harness as his tether rewound as
he was pulled quickly towards the shuttle. "Al, do a
proximity sweep."

Liam saw Paul using his wand to jet towards the
shuttle before a bright light exploded across his
vision. Then nothing.

* * *

Liam drifted in that nether region, neither
asleep nor awake. The bed was so comfortable,
like floating on silk. What day was it? What time
was his alarm set for? How much longer could he
sleep? He tried to peek one eye open to look at
the clock on his nightstand, hoping it was early
enough to go back to sleep. Everything was black.
Had he opened his eye or just dreamed he had?

His conscious mind started to fight the sleep,
but he was groggy, real groggy. What day was
it? Saturday, he remembered. He had gone out

drinking with his friends Friday night. He kicked himself. After the bender he threw when he pinned his wings, he swore he would never do that again. Spending half the night hunched over a toilet bowl was enough of a lesson. He felt so groggy, he knew this would be a bad one. Why did he do it again?

A moment later he realized he hadn't. He was going to go out, but then Paul had called him. He had gone into space. There was a satellite. A spacewalk. A bright flash.

Liam fought the sleep. He tried to move, but couldn't feel anything. He was floating. He tried to move some more and then the pain hit. Now he was awake, but he hurt everywhere. He forced his eyes open, but still could not see anything. Was he blind? Then he saw stars. Not figuratively, but real stars. He watched as stars slid across his view and then light from the moon flooded in. He was floating inside the shuttle. The shuttle was in a slow spin, showing him stars and then a portion of the moon through the open doors. And then stars again.

Liam managed to reach out and hold the ceiling of the shuttle, stabilizing himself. The shuttle was dark. No lights shown on the console. 'That can't be good,' Liam thought. What was that flash? Was it an explosion? He hadn't heard anything. Can you hear an explosion in space? he wondered. Where was Paul? WHERE WAS PAUL?

Bracing himself, Liam tried to look around the inside of the shuttle. The movement hurt and he had to wait for the shuttle to point towards the moon so he had enough light to see. Paul was not in the shuttle. A wave of panic threatened to overwhelm him, but he forced it down. One step at a time, he told himself. Find Paul. How?

Liam moved painfully to the open door and was caught by his tether. The tether! Find Paul's tether. He waited for the shuttle to spin towards the light again and found Paul's tether anchored in the shuttle. It disappeared out the open door. He reached over and grabbed the tether. Please let Paul be on the other side, he thought as he gently pulled. There was solid resistance. Yes! He pulled slowly, feeling the weight on the other end. And then it stopped. He pulled harder, but the tether was stuck. He would have to go out and get him.

Slowly, painfully, he moved to the open door and tried to push out. His tether stopped him. He tried again. Nothing. He tried pulling on the tether, but like a stuck seat belt, it would not move. He would have to unhook his tether to go outside. He remembered Paul's warning about floating away in space. He would just have to hold on. He unhooked his tether and slowly climbed out of the shuttle. Once outside the doors, the shuttle did not have anything to hold onto, it was all smooth curves. Liam pulled himself hand over hand on Paul's tether. It was wrapped around the shuttle.

Now Paul is the tether ball, Liam thought as he carefully climbed up the tether.

He found Paul pressed against the bottom of the shuttle. "Paul, Paul, can you hear me?" There was no response. Paul felt limp and Liam could not see inside his visor. Assume he is alive, Liam told himself. Carefully he braced himself against the shuttle and lifted Paul free. Liam's feet drifted away from the shuttle and again Liam almost panicked as he realized he and Paul were drifting away. But then he remembered Paul's tether. It had better hold, he thought as he carefully maneuvered them back towards the shuttle by pulling on the tether.

An eternity later, he and Paul were inside the shuttle. "Al, close the doors," Liam instructed. Nothing happened. He really was not that surprised. When the shuttle turned again so he could see, he reached over and activated the door controls. Nothing happened. He tried again. Nothing. This is not good, Liam thought. And then he noticed the icon on his helmet was yellow. He was using up his oxygen. One step at a time, he told himself as part of his brain was screaming that he was going to die. He needed to close the shuttle doors.

The escape pod had a manual door opener. The shuttle must also, he reasoned. He searched the doorway until he found a spot above the open door that looked like the same access hatch on the escape pod. He tried to open it, but it would not budge. Where did Paul store that tool he had used on the escape pod? He thought back and remembered Paul leaning into the back before climbing in. Liam searched the back, finding access panels he had not noticed. The second one held the tool. Carefully, he held it up to the access and pushed. It opened. He then engaged the tool and cranked, watching the doors close ever so slowly.

By the time the doors closed, his icon was flashing yellow. Not good, not good, Liam thought. With the doors closed, the inside of the shuttle was pitch black. By feel, he manually pulled the front seats back into the upright position and floated Paul's limp body into his seat and fastened him in with the restraints. He sat in the pilot's seat and fastened the seat, watching his flashing icon intently. On the moon, shuttle oxygen had transferred automatically into his suit as soon as he sat down. The icon continued to blink yellow. He shifted around in the seat, wondering if he needed a better connection. But the icon continued to blink yellow.

It's not working! He wondered if he was actually having trouble breathing or if it was his imagination. Either way, if he did not fix this soon, it would be real enough. He tried to look at the console. His suit optics were not adjusting to the dark. Remembering that even the shuttle retained some of the characteristics of the Honda, he reached overhead and felt the ceiling, searching for a light. He found something, and pushed it repeatedly until a soft glow filled the cockpit.

His suit icon was flashing red. He knew he wasn't imagining breathing hard now. Where did Paul say life support was? He needed a glove compartment with an owner's manual in it. But the shuttle did not copy the Honda in that respect. He searched the console, but all the displays were dead, not even a flashing cursor. He was about to give up when he wondered whether life support would have a manual back up, like the doors? If it did, Paul had never shown him. Where would it be? He found that he was holding his breath, every couple of breaths, trying to extend his time.

Where would it be? The air came from the seats, he reasoned. So, if there is a backup, it is in the seats. He turned and examined Paul's seat, pressing and pulling on anything that looked like a latch. Suddenly, a panel on the side of the seat opened. Liam reached inside and pulled out a short orange hose with a flat surface on the end. He searched his seat and found an identical one. How did it attach? There was nothing on his suit that looked like an attachment. His icon flashed once more and then turned solid red. Liam gasped. He couldn't breathe. The suit seemed to constrict him as he gasped for air that wasn't there. His vision started to fade as his lungs fought for air.

He pushed the flat part of the hose against his chest and air filled his suit. He gasped, panting for air as his vision came back. He could not get enough. Then he remembered Paul. He reached over and pressed the other hose against Paul's chest, making sure that it stuck and hoping that it gave Paul air and that Paul was still alive.

Liam let himself have the luxury of sitting and breathing for a minute before he tackled the next problem. He had to activate the communications panel and contact the Delorians. Then hope they would arrive before life support ran out. But hadn't Paul and Liam performed the lunar rescue because the Delorians were too far away to assist? In that case, he would have to get the propulsion system back on line and fly back to Earth. But flying the damaged shuttle did not seem like a viable option. The ship seemed dead.

He decided to work on the console and see what came up. He needed to get some computer back on line, that was for sure. Although there may be some manual controls, he was certain they were beyond his ability to use, assuming he even found them. He worried about Paul. Was he alive? The cockpit did not have any air, so Liam could not open Paul's suit to check on him. He would have to hope for the best and try to get the shuttle working. If he could reactivate Al, then Al could fly them back to Earth.

Liam played with the console, trying to find

some switch that would turn it on or perhaps reboot the computer. He knew there was some power left since the dome light had come on. As Liam worked, he realized how much he hurt. When he had been active, he had pushed the pain away. Now that he was just sitting, the pain came creeping back. He hurt everywhere, but the worst was the throbbing headache. He tried to ignore it. He was having trouble concentrating and felt his arms getting sluggish. Maybe if I just rest for a minute, it will pass, he thought, although part of him said that was a bad idea. But in the end, he closed his eyes and consciousness slipped away.

# CHAPTER FIVE

Liam opened his eyes. He was lying in bed, his alarm clock beeping insistently. He rolled over and slapped the snooze button, realizing he could not stay in bed much longer. Sunlight was already streaming in through his bedroom window. Five minutes, he told himself. I just need five more minutes, then I'll get up.

He stretched under the covers and realized he did not hurt anywhere. That was good. It had taken a while to heal after that fateful trip in the shuttle. Liam replayed the events as he lay there.

*  *  *

He woke up inside a recovery pod. He had not known it at the time, all he knew was there was a clear panel four inches from his face and he could not move. He would have panicked or gotten claustrophobic, but the drugs kept everything hazy. His next memory had been the lid raising. It was bright and a Delorian was looking down at him. It was Sally.

"May I help you out of the recovery pod," she asked.

When he muttered yes, she reached down and effortlessly picked him up like a baby and turned and placed him on a nearby table that jutted out of the adjacent wall. The table was surprisingly soft. The walls and ceiling above him were a light gray. "Am I at your base?" Liam asked, his voice rasping in his throat.

"You are," Sally replied.

Liam lay there, trying to piece together what happened. Sally just waited. Slowly, Liam's memory started to reassemble the events: the shuttle, the spacewalk, the blinding light.

"Paul," Liam gasped. "Paul, is he okay?"

"He will be," Sally said.

"Where is he?"

"He is here," Sally said, gesturing behind her.

Liam painfully turned his head and saw four other pods lining the far wall. The one Sally was pointing to was closed. Indecipherable lights flickered on a panel above it.

"What happened?"

"Paul will tell you," Sally said. "But first I must test you," she added as she placed a pair of dark glasses over his eyes. Lights and patterns swirled in the glasses and Liam closed his eyes as a wave of nausea swept over him. "Open your eyes," Sally instructed and Liam reluctantly complied. The patterns continued, but the nausea passed. After a minute, she removed the glasses and had Liam raise his arms and legs one at a time. It hurt, but not alarmingly so.

"Tell me what happened," Liam repeated.

"Paul will, when you wake up," Sally said.

"I'm not sleepy..." is all that Liam said, before he fell back asleep. Liam had some vague memories of talking and walking, but it was all hazy and disjointed. His next clear memory started with Sally speaking.

"He can hear you now..." Sally was saying.

"Liam? Liam, can you hear me?" Paul was asking.

Liam was suddenly wide awake as all the memories of the shuttle trip flooded back. He shook his head and looked around the room. He was sitting in a reclining chair in another small gray room. Across from him, Paul was sitting in another recliner. Sally stood off to the side. There was nothing else in the room.

"Good morning," Paul said when he realized Liam was awake.

Liam glanced around, getting his bearings. "What happened? Are you okay?"

"Thanks to you," Paul responded. "You saved my life."

Liam thought back. "I remember the flash, and getting you back into the shuttle. I don't remember getting back here."

"You wouldn't. You were unconscious. We both were," Paul said. "You hooked us up to life support."

"We saw the flash," Sally interjected. "You saved me when my escape pod crashed on the Moon. Now, I got to return the favor by saving you."

"We both had bad concussions," Paul continued the story. "And an assortment of other injuries. Fortunately, the Delorians are very knowledgeable of human physic and are quite adept at healing us."

Liam nodded. That made sense. "What happened? Before, I mean. Were we attacked? I remember you yelling and then a bright flash."

"Proximity mine," Paul explained. "When I examined the satellite, I realized it was not damaged by a solar flare. It was fired upon. I figured it was a trap. And we walked right into it. Sorry," he said to Liam. "That's the second time I dragged you out to get shot at, so to speak."

"You promised me an adventure," Liam chuckled.

"Yes, but I did not mean that big of an adventure," Paul said. "What I want to know is how did you save us both after the mine went off. I don't remember anything after that?"

Liam proceeded to tell Paul and Sally what he

had done until he had passed out. "I'm so glad I showed you how to operate the shuttle," Paul said, when Liam had finished his story.

"How is the shuttle?" Liam asked.

"It was not recoverable," Sally replied.

"I'm going to have to go to the dealer and get a new one," Paul said with a laugh. "They have to customize them for us humans, you know."

"How long does that take," Liam asked. Then his stomach tightened. "What day is it?" It was Friday night when they took off. He prayed that there was still enough time to get him back before Monday's roll call.

"It is Thursday," Paul said.

"Thursday! It can't be Thursday. I'm AWOL. I've missed four days!" Liam was in a panic.

"It's Thursday, the following week," Paul said. "But you are not AWOL. We have a cover story for you."

* * *

The bedside alarm rang again and Liam hit it as he rolled out of bed. Yea, they had a cover story all right. He was involved in a hit and run accident and sustained a concussion. He did not remember the accident or anything leading up to it, nor his time at the hospital until he woke up. That kept remembering his cover story very easy. The Delorians had planted the appropriate medical records in the hospital computer and then sent them to the military. No one was the wiser. The problem was that with the concussion and missed time, he had been dropped from the flight rotation. Now he was waiting for a military doctor to clear him for flight status and hoping he could get back into the flight training program before he fell too far behind his classmates. In the meantime, he was being assigned meaningless admin jobs.

Halfheartedly, Liam got dressed and had a bowl of cereal for breakfast before heading out the door. When he stepped out on the porch, he stopped and stared. Parked in front of his house was a gold Honda. Paul had talked with Liam several times over the last couple months, but all of the conversations were benign, asking how Liam was progressing and what he was doing at work. Paul was very strict about not talking about anything more detailed over an unsecure line. Liam wondered if something had changed.

As Liam walked up to the Honda, the passenger window rolled down. "We need to talk," Paul said without preamble.

"Nothing ever good comes after those words. Although I usually hear them from my girlfriend," Liam responded.

"You have a girlfriend?"

"No. Not anymore. That's what I mean."

Paul smiled. "Well, you are right. Get in."

Liam climbed into the car and closed the door. "I have to report in thirty-five minutes," Liam said, looking at his watch.

"I'll make this quick," Paul said. "The Delorians believe the recent attacks are a precurser for a much larger attack."

"An attack against the Delorians?"

"No. Earth."

"Aliens are going to attack Earth?" Liam asked.

"Yes. And the Delorians want us to help defend Earth."

Liam tried to understand what he just heard. Aliens attacking Earth? That was straight out of science fiction. But with Paul, everything was science fiction. What aliens? Why were they attacking? What did they want? How would they attack? When? The questions were unending.

Even after having travelled to the Moon and walking in space, Liam was still having trouble processing an alien presence on Earth. Liam watched two of his neighbors walk by the car, oblivious to the conversation he was having. How could the Earth be about to be attacked by aliens? Liam looked back at Paul, who was just waiting for him to respond.

Liam finally managed to gather his thoughts. "I don't think the military could defeat your shuttle, let alone a fighter," Liam finally responded. "How do the Delorians think we can defend Earth,"

"They will provide us with fighters. The ones you saw in the cavern. We just need to train the pilots."

"We?"

"Yes. I need to put together a squadron of pilots and I want you to be my X.O."

"Me? I'm a Lieutenant, Junior Grade in the Coast Guard! We don't even have squadrons. And I'm still in flight training. Heck, I'm not even in flight training now. You need a Commander, at least."

Paul held up his hand. "You don't understand. This will be a black-ops mission. No one other than the pilots will know about it. That's why you will be the perfect X.O. This is how you liaison for the Delorians. And besides, you won't freak out about the aliens."

"I don't know. I'm feeling pretty freaked out right now."

"That's because I threw you a curve ball."

"All you throw are curve balls," Liam protested. "You haven't thrown me a straight pitch yet."

Paul chuckled.

"How do you propose that 'we' recruit and train a squadron of fighter pilots with no one finding out?" Liam continued.  "It doesn't sound like something we can do on the weekends."

"Actually, the military is the perfect place for confidential orders. With the help of the Delorians,

I already have black-op status and can create any orders I want. Right now, a Colonel at Eglin Air Force Base is obtaining a secure location for our training. I need you to identify potential recruits. They need to have some flight training, but not too much where they are inflexible. Flying a space fighter is very different than flying an aircraft. I will issue them orders to report for testing. If they pass the initial tests, then we will recruit them for training."

"How will I do all that? I'm only a Lieutenant Junior Grade."

"You will receive TDY orders from your command and then another set of orders from me, which will let you do anything we need you to do."

"You can do that?"

"Not me," Paul said. "The Delorians. There is not a computer on Earth they can't hack. The orders will all be legit on the computers. And since they will be classified, very few people will check on them."

"So, I won't be able to finish my flight training?" Liam asked.

"I think you are losing sight of the big picture here. Do you want to fly a plane or a spaceship?"

Liam stared out the window. "We really are going to be attacked by aliens?"

"Hard to imagine, isn't it," Paul said. "But then, they probably thought that on December 7th, at

Pearl Harbor."

"True," Liam agreed. He paused while he considered what Paul had told him. He remembered watching a movie about Pearl Harbor. A beautiful Sunday morning, blue sky, people laughing and playing, and then disbelief as Japanese planes dive bombed. He imagined the same thing today, but with alien fighters. "Okay, I'm in," he finally said. "What do you want me to do?"

"First, I'm going to get you to work on time," Paul said. "Later today your command will call you in to give you special TDY orders. You will act as surprised as they are. Then you will report to me as specified in your orders. I will fill you in on the details later."

With that Paul drove Liam to his duty station and dropped him off. "See you soon," Paul said as he rolled up the window and drove away, leaving Liam standing in front of the building, wondering what was going to happen next. He was not going to have to wait long to find out.

# CHAPTER SIX

One month later, one hundred and thirty-seven pilots in civilian clothing milled around inside a gym at Eglin Air Force Base. Many of the pilots knew each other and were clustering around in groups, asking each other why they had been ordered here at 0800 hours on a Saturday morning and generally complaining about the military screwing around with their weekend.

Liam, also wearing civilian clothing, walked among them, directing them to one end of the gym where rectangular folding tables were set up end to end. Folding metal chairs were placed six feet apart and laptops were sitting on the tables. Each laptop had a tape across the top with a name hand written on it. This was the third time and the third base where he and Paul had run these tests.

Assembling the group had not been difficult. Paul had loaded an app on Liam's phone that appeared to be a dog-fighting game. The game started with biplanes and then progressed up to F-19's. The graphics were crisp and the game was easy to play on a smart phone. Liam shared the app with other pilots on base, on social media, at the Officer's Club, or anywhere else he met pilots and encouraged them to share the link to the game with their friends. The game ran a preliminary evaluation on the player, reporting the results to the Delorians. Promising candidates received orders to show up at a test site, never knowing how they were selected.

Slowly the pilots wandered over to the tables and located their assigned laptop. Liam moved to the front of the group and called out, "Attention on deck."

Even wearing civilian clothing, the effect was immediate. One hundred and thirty-seven individuals suddenly jumped to attention, eyes and backs straight. After the initial scraping of chairs, silence filled the gym, broken only by the sound of one set of footsteps approaching the front. An older black man in a blue, pin-striped business suit walked to the front of the group and turned to survey the pilots standing at attention. At six-feet tall, he looked reasonably fit. He was bald, with a short cropped gray beard. He could have been military, except for the beard, and the suit was too nice. He looked like he had just stepped out of a court room, or perhaps a board room.

The pilots stayed at attention, wondering who this civilian was and what authority he had. "As you were," the civilian finally said, "be seated." When the noise of scraping chairs stopped, the man continued.

"I'm sure you are all curious why you were ordered here this morning. Let me explain. We are conducting tests to determine how your training affects your neural pathways. Spatial awareness. Reaction times. Flexibility versus rigid cognition. Situational awareness, as you have heard repeatedly during your training. The scientists would explain this in detail that would put us all to sleep. The bottom line is that we are conducting cognitive tests of personnel in the beginning of flight training through seasoned pilots to identify cognitive changes.

"Our flight systems are getting more and more complicated. Training is taking longer. The eggheads are trying to develop a better operator/system interface that enhances our efficiency in training and your ability to operate the systems in a high stress combat setting. Regardless of how stupid you might think these tests are, they have the potential of affecting future training and perhaps even your training. So, pay attention and give them your best effort.

"When I tell you, you will open your laptop and log in. You will confirm the personal information already entered into your laptop and follow the instructions provided. Each of these laptops has been programmed to administer a battery of tests.

The programs are interactive and will proceed along different paths depending upon your responses. Some of these will seem very simple, some very confusing, some downright stupid." That elicited a couple of chuckles.

"These tests are not so much about knowledge, but about your reactions. How you interface with the program. When you have completed the series of tests, close the computer. I will conduct a short exit interview with each of you and then you may leave. Some of you may be requested to return for more testing. Most of you will just chalk this up to another nonsensical requirement of the military." Another round of chuckles. "You should be out of here before noon."

"As with most new things in the military," the man continued, "this meeting is classified." Suddenly, everyone paid more attention. "Although these tests will seem simplistic, the programs running them are cutting-edge technology. You are authorized to tell anyone who asks that you were asked to participate in some cognitive testing and that it was a stupid waste of time. But from the time you open your laptop, until you step out that door, everything else is classified and will not leave this room. Is that understood?"

A chorus of "Yes, Sir," resounded across the gym.

"Okay. Open your laptops."

* * *

One week later, thirty-four pilots filed into a classroom at Eglin Air Force base on a Saturday morning. There was a pot of coffee on a back table with assorted pastries. As was typical in the military, they were ordered to report at 0800 hours for a meeting they were told would begin at 0830.

Untypically, they were ordered to report in civvies, not uniforms. They spent thirty minutes milling around the coffee and pastries before slowly making their way to their seats. They had not been told why they were ordered here and complained about missing another nice beach day for bureaucratic nonsense. Some were stationed outside the Gulf Coast and had received last minute TDY orders directing them to report to Eglin AFB. Their complaints were tempered by the fact their orders would allow them to play on the beach for a couple of days before returning to their duty stations.

Several wondered whether they were about to do more stupid cognitive testing, like they had done earlier, with the consensus being that the military was once again proving its incompetence. Their complaining became more pronounced as 0830 came and went and no one started the meeting. 0840 came and went. 0850, still nothing.

Some of the pilots were beginning to pace around the room.  At 0851 Liam, who had been blending in with the group, suddenly called out, "Attention on deck." Everyone snapped to attention. Those carrying coffee or doughnuts furtively looked for a place to put down their coffee or held it in their hands, hoping no one noticed.

The same gray bearded man they had met before walked to the front of the classroom. This time he was wearing a gray suit and once again the pilots wondered who he was. He had never introduced himself during the last meeting. He stared pointedly around the room before he spoke.

"Sit down." Chairs scraped as the pilots sat. A few pilots quickly darted for their seats. "This is a classified briefing," the man began when everyone had been seated. "Nothing, and I mean nothing of what we talk about today can leave this room." There was no hint of joking or levity in his demeanor. The pilots glanced at each other, then back to the front.

"Based upon your test results, you have been chosen to participate in a top-secret experimental program involving revolutionary technology in an advanced aerial platform. This program is voluntary. I will not order you to participate. It will be rigorous and require great sacrifice. If you choose to volunteer, you will receive classified TDY orders. That is all your command will know. You will ship out to a secure location for a minimum of six months. You will have very limited contact with anyone outside of this program. No girlfriends, no boyfriends, no family. All outside communication will be monitored and censored as necessary. The training will be rigorous. It will be dangerous. You will not be coddled by flight instructors. You will be the flight instructors as we develop this interface. If the program succeeds, you will see combat. And many of you will die." The man paused to let his words sink in.

"You joined the United States military. All branches are represented among you today: Air Force, Navy, Marines, Army and Coast Guard. Many people join the military for the benefits, considering it just another job. Some use it as a stepping stone to a cushy civilian job flying for Delta. Those people don't think of the possibility of war. And then there are the few who join the military to defend our country.

"Ladies and Gentlemen, there is an enemy planning an attack on us. Even now they are massing at our doorstep. If they succeed, it will affect everyone. It will make 9-11 or Pearl Harbor seem insignificant. Right now, we can't touch them. But with the technology and training we will be putting together in the next six months, we will have a chance to hit them in a fashion they will never expect.

"I am asking for a great sacrifice from you. But I can offer you an experience beyond your wildest dreams, and an opportunity to serve your country like no one else. I can also provide absolute assurance that what you are doing is vitally important to our very survival. I am not overstating the threat against us."

The man paused as he gazed across the assembled pilots. "There is little more I can tell you at this time. If you decide to volunteer, report to hangar J here at Eglin at 0600 hours Monday. Wear your flight suits. You may bring one standard duffel with personal belongings. Bring Class B Uniform and civvies. Moderate climate clothing is all you will need.  All electronics, including watches, phones, tablets and computers will be collected before you leave. They will be returned to you after being modified to ensure they do not send out any signals. If that offends you, then don't bring them."

"Any questions?"

There was silence in the room. Finally, one pilot raised his hand.

"Yes."

"What will we be flying? Can you tell us?"

"No," the man replied. "However, I know you all come from different backgrounds, are at different points of your flight training and fly different air frames. Some of you fly rotary wing frames, some props, some jets. I can tell you that if you complete the training, you will fly an advanced fighter with capabilities beyond your wildest imagination. Based upon the testing you have completed, the powers that be feel confidant you will all qualify."

Another hand. "This is a black-ops operation?"

"Yes. And not to put too fine an edge on it, if anyone breathes a word of this briefing, they will not see the light of day until the mission is completed. And then they will be court-martialed."

Assuming there was anyone left to court-martial them, Liam thought as he watched from the side of the room.

There were a few more questions, but no further substantive information was provided.

"If you join this mission and have any logistical issues that need to be resolved, such as leases or other duties, contact Lieutenant Turner here." He motioned towards Liam. "He will give you his card as you leave. You will find he can make most problems disappear."

The man looked around the room. "I hope to see you all on Monday. You are dismissed."

After the pilots left the room to contemplate their decisions, Liam and Paul walked over to Paul's Honda, which was parked right outside the classroom.

"What do you think?" Liam asked Paul as they climbed into the Honda. "Do you think they will volunteer?"

"I think most will," Paul replied. "The Delorians

predict an 18% attrition rate. They have vetted them pretty closely. They have their official records, and more importantly everything they have done electronically, whether it be social media, phone, text or email. All in all, have a pretty good profile on each of them.

"Why did you delay the start of the meeting?"

"Part of the testing," Paul replied. "The Delorians wanted to watch their reactions. Don't ask me why. I don't understand most of what the Delorians do."

"You did not tell them much, yet you're asking them to drop everything for a least six months," Liam said.

"It worked with you," Paul noted.

"You promised me the Moon and proved you could deliver."

"And I promised them a fighter, combat and a meaningful assignment."

"You promised to get them killed," Liam said.

"No one your age believes they are mortal. They will take that as a challenge," Paul said. "Make sure to keep me posted on any contacts you have with them," Paul added as he drove away.

# CHAPTER SEVEN

Between 0530 and 0600 hours Monday morning, thirty pilots reported to hangar J on Eglin Air Force Base. There they discovered Lt. Turner was LTJG Liam Turner with the USCG, an O-2, not a Navy O-3 that many had guessed. Liam had worked with many of them over the weekend resolving various issues arising from their sudden departure. Of the four who did not arrive, one had rejected the offer and the other three had requested an extension of time to take care of personal matters. Paul cut them from the program as being insufficiently motivated.

At 0630 hours the group marched over to a nearby C-130 warming up on the tarmac. After getting their gear stowed and receiving a briefing from the loading NCO, they were wheels up. An hour later they landed. The ramp dropped and they deplaned. The C-130 took off immediately, forcing them to crouch against the prop wash. Looking around, the pilots realized they were standing on a deserted runway surrounded by a pine forest. In the distance stood a lone hangar. They hefted their duffels and Lt. Turner led them across the runway towards the hangar.

"This runway hasn't been used in years," Chuck Williams, one of the pilots said, as he eyed the grass peeking through the crevasses of the old runway.

"Would not be safe for a jet," Sarah Tenneson, a pilot training for jets, remarked. "Would suck all this into the intakes."

"That would ruin your day," someone else replied.

"I bet this hasn't been used since World War II," Chuck Williams said as he eyed the hangar. It was a large, three story, metal building with faded green paint. Multiple telescoping bay doors lined the front of the building.

"It was probably pretty impressive in its day," someone remarked. "You could fit a bunch of planes in there."

Lt. Turner led them to a regular door at one end of the hangar. It opened with a squeak of old hinges. They filed into the hanger. The inside was cavernous, lit only by light seeping in through a row of dirty windows lining the top of the walls thirty feet above them. Lt. Turner flicked a switch on the wall. Light filled the hangar. It was empty, except at one side unpainted wood framed walls ran down the length of the hangar. The walls were only twelve feet tall, leaving a large gap to the ceiling of the hangar. The smell of fresh lumber filled the air.

"This will be our temporary base of operations," Lt. Turner began, his voice echoing in the empty space. "It's not much to look at, but it will serve our purpose for the time being." He pointed to a door on the right side of the new construction. "Over there are barracks. You will find bunks and lockers where you can stow your belongings. On the far end of the barracks are showers and restrooms. The living quarters are unisex. You are adults and all officers. Act like it and make suitable arrangements. That is the way it will be when we go into the field, so you might as well get used to it now."

"This is not the field?" someone in the back muttered.

Lt. Turner ignored the comment. "On the left," he pointed to the other door, "is a classroom and break room. Our initial training will be done there." He paused before continuing. "You have fifteen minutes to stow your gear. You will find your names on your bunks and lockers. Then report back here in your P.T. uniform. After P.T., we will have breakfast and then get to work. Dismissed."

P.T. consisted of the usual sit-ups, pushups and then jogging around the airfield a couple times in formation. After P.T., they showered and met back in the main part of the hangar wearing their flight suits. Liam pointed to a large box in the corner and said, "Help yourself to breakfast."

The pilots walked suspiciously over to the box and looked inside.

"I don't believe it, MRE's," one pilot said. With a lot of complaining, they all grabbed some MRE's and started trading for their favorites as they sat in groups on the hangar floor. Barely twenty minutes later Lt. Turner directed them to the classroom.

The classroom was unpainted plasterboard walls about twelve feet tall and a flat, unpainted ceiling. Three rows of ten reclining chairs faced the front of the room where a 72" flat screen TV was mounted. Two recliners were in the front on either side of the TV. Next to each recliner was a square gray box about a foot on each side, which looked like a heavy-duty storage container.

The pilots continued to complain as they entered the room, until they noticed the gray-haired man was standing in the front of the classroom. The comments quickly died out as they made their ways to the chairs, wondering if they should sit down or stand at attention. The man motioned for them to sit.

"I'm sorry I did not join you for P.T.," the man said. "As much fun as I'm sure it would have been, I have no intention of competing with a bunch of twenty-somethings." That elicited a few chuckles in the group. "Some of you have been asking who I am. You can call me Captain Paul. Lt. Turner here is my X.O. You can go to him for any issues you have. Some of you are Lieutenants, a few are Captains, or O-2's and O-3's for those of you who are in the Navy or Coast Guard side of the house. For purposes of this operation, Lt. Turner outranks all of you. And each of you will be called trainees, until you earn your wings to fly my birds."

"You are probably wondering what you have gotten into," Captain Paul continued. "I promised you cutting-edge technology and you find yourselves in a World War II hangar on a deserted airstrip in these palatial surroundings," he motioned towards the walls of the classroom. "These are temporary quarters and I will admit they were put together rather hastily. The tech, however, was not. We are going to get right to it. Open the container next to you and pull out the contents."

The trainees all leaned over and opened the containers next to them. Inside was a pair of goggles, about the size of a pair of swim goggles, and a pair of blue gloves that looked like the cloth version of latex surgical gloves. There were also a pair of cloth booties.

"Slip the booties over your boots," Captain Paul instructed. Once the trainees had all complied, he said, "Now put on the goggles with the little tabs on the side hanging down, not up. Make sure they are comfortable. You will be wearing them for several hours." He gave them a few moments to adjust the goggles. The goggles were clear, so everyone could still see him. He was putting on a pair of goggles as he spoke. "See these tabs," he said, motioning to two tabs hanging down on either side of his goggles. "Press these against the bone behind your ear." He waited for everyone to comply, then added, "Now slip on the gloves." When he saw that everyone had their gloves on, he said, "Recline your chairs and sit back with your hands on the armrests."

Captain Paul walked over and sat in the recliner at the side of the room. "Close your eyes and listen carefully." The sounds of insects and birds filled their heads, although it did not seem to come from their ears. "Open your eyes," Captain Paul's voice filled their heads. "They were all standing in a large circle in a grassy field. Birds flew overhead, while the sun beat down from a blue sky. White clouds floated in the distance.

"Holy sh..." one of them said, catching himself in mid-sentence.

"Yes, everything you say can be heard by the rest of us," Captain Paul said. "In fact, you don't have to say it out loud. A whisper or even sub-vocalization will be sufficient. Now, move your hands around." People started moving their hands and then stared at them like some strange appendage. "Now pick up your feet." A couple people fell down, to the laughter of the others. "I said pick them up, not step forward." The trainees who fell, struggled to get up. When they finally succeeded, Captain Paul continued.

"Welcome to virtual reality like you have never experienced before. This is the introductory program to get you used to the concept." The trainees looked around. The VR was seamless. They could see blades of grass and spot grasshoppers jumping from blade to blade. There were no glitches or blurring as they moved their heads. Looking at their fellow trainees was the same as looking at them normally. Moving their hands, moved them seamlessly in VR.

"As impressive as the visual rendering is," Captain Paul continued, "it is not the impressive part of this program. Each of you has a personal A.I. assigned to you. A.I. does not mean artificial intelligence, it means adaptive intelligence, which is much, much more. Scientists, and science fiction writers for that matter, have long debated on where the line will be between a computer program and sentient life. When you have finished this program, you will be asking yourselves the same question. Your A.I. will assist you in the training program and will be your co-pilot when you fly my fighters. They can independently fly the ships. Get to know them. Find out their name. Treat them as your equal."

Someone chuckled in the VR.

Captain Paul paused. "You laugh. One of the most important reasons we chose you to join this program and not seasoned pilots, is that we needed folks with some flight training, but who were not too rigidly locked in to their believes or reflexes. In the next twenty-four hours your world will change completely. Some of your core beliefs will be challenged. What I ask of each of you is to approach each event with an open mind. Pay attention to all that you see and hear and do not make any judgements until you have all the evidence before you. If you will do that, and I believe you all can, then you will complete this program."

"Today will be fun and games, playing with this VR program and meeting your A.I. It is also your first test, whether you can adapt to this new information, this new reality. By the way, the A.I.'s believe they are sentient. Quite frankly, I agree with them. Treat them with respect. This is not SIRI or ALEXA, this is their great, great, great, great grandchild. Whether you believe they are sentient or not, they will be your co-pilots and can save your lives. You will need to learn their capabilities and their limitations."

# CHAPTER EIGHT

Liam was taking the training along with everyone else. He was physically sitting in the recliner across from Paul, but on VR he was standing with the group of pilots out in the field. When Paul finished his speech, the field and other pilots disappeared, to be replaced by the view of the underground cavern with the fighters floating in it.

"Wow. I did not expect that," he whispered.

"I thought you would like to start with something you were already acquainted with," a familiar voice spoke in his ear.

"Al, is that you?" Liam asked.

"Yes, it is."

"What are you doing in here? Aren't you in the shuttle?"

"I am in both places. Paul thought you would be more comfortable training with me since we had already met."

"Are you talking to the others as well?"

"I have a subroutine talking to them," Al said. "They are not being introduced to the fighter yet. Too much in one sitting. They are playing video games, to get them used to the program." Suddenly the view changed and Liam was in a virtual game of Space Invaders, but instead of playing the game from a computer or joystick, he was in the cockpit of the ship. "This will get them used to space," Al said. "Of course, what they are being told is that we are using this program to work on their gaming reflexes and give them time to adjust to their A.I. However, after tonight's demonstration, they will be seeing this."

The view changed. Now Liam was standing on an airfield. But instead of airplanes lined up on the tarmac, it was thirty Delorian fighters. The other pilots, or their virtual selves, were all grouped around one fighter with a stereotypical looking flight instructor in a flight suit, complete with Captain's bars, standing in front pointing out the characteristics of the fighter.

"Ha," Liam laughed. "I had a flight instructor just like him."

"You can join this group if you want," Al said.

"No," Liam responded. "He was a pain in the butt. Besides, I prefer the realistic tour."

In a blink of an eye, Liam found himself back in the cavern with the floating fighters.

"I won't repeat what Paul showed you on the fighter already," Al began the lesson. "Let me start with what he did not point out. But first, I must object to your calling this an 'X-Wing' fighter," Al said. "I have accessed the X-wing footage on the web and there is no comparison. The Star Wars' fighter is a crude, limited vehicle that..."

"It has wings that form an X," Liam interrupted. "It's an X-Wing."

Liam could have sworn he heard Al sigh with exasperation. "Those wings," Al continued, "are four fixed pilons that extend out from the rear of the craft and sweep forward. They house crucial flight control, shield, armament and sensor modules that require some distance from the main body of the fighter. They are swept forward to provide the shield modules with optimal placement to protect the entire craft. And they only resemble and X in the most abstract sense..."

"It is a lot sleeker than an X-wing," Liam said.

"True," Al said. "The Delorians favor a spherical design with rounded edges in all of their craft. You won't see any harsh lines or jutting surfaces, like you saw on the fighter that attacked us. Now, the Delorian fighter is two point seven times larger than the shuttle. The cockpit sits one third back into the ship and can be configured to seat one or two occupants. Like the shuttle, the fighter has what you call a sunroof. This is the only access port and it can dock with other Delorian ships, providing access to and from the fighter when the fighter does not land inside another ship. The outer surface is a composite adaptive material that can auto-repair to a degree."

Liam found himself starting to glaze over as Al launched into the detailed specifications of the fighter. However, he perked up again when Al described the weapons systems. "The fighter has a phased-array system like the shuttle, but much more powerful. It fires off all four pylons at these points here," markers lit up on the tips of the pilons, "and alternates frequency so it is harder for shields to block. The firing points have a 220-degree firing range, so you don't have to be facing your target to fire, unlike the shuttle. The shields have to retract some when firing the phased-array, so the firing points will be vulnerable to attack while you are firing. And they pull a lot of power, so you have to juggle your power requirements between shields, firing and thrust. You probably also want to save some power for life support."

"Was that a joke?" Liam asked. "Did you actually make a joke?"

"Your humor is not that difficult to emulate."

"Oh my, a comic A.I." Liam almost said computer, but caught himself, remembering Paul's warning about the A.I.'s being touchy on the subject.

Al ignored Liam's comment and continued the

briefing. "The fighter can also carry two-hundred thousand darts." Images of the darts appeared in the air as Al talked, along with a list of their specifications floating next to them. The darts were about the size of a large magic marker and about the same shape, except they were smooth. "The darts are what you fired at the Red Force fighter."

"And missed," Liam added.

"True," Al said. "But it distracted the fighter so Paul could hit it with the phased-array. A very effective combination and quite remarkable considering that I had been rendered unconscious."

"The destructive power of the darts is their speed and the corresponding kinetic energy they deliver to a target. The downside, as you remember, is that they can be avoided depending on the distance to the target. Also, because of their small size, there is a limit to how much energy can be transferred and hence how much potential damage they can cause. We will discuss this in much further detail later.

"The fighter can be configured to carry two missiles, one on each side of the forward fuselage. They are larger and much longer than the darts, but otherwise look about the same. They pack a much greater punch, as you put it. They are designed for ship killing, not for fighter-to-fighter conflict. Unlike the darts, which are similar to your bullets, the missiles can seek out their target. You can fire and forget or you can control their entire flight. However, the missiles have issues also. They can be jammed, intercepted and shielded against. We will ..."

"... Discuss this in much further detail later," Liam finished Al's sentence.

"There is one other weapon system on this fighter. Mounted here at the rear of the fighter, between the top and bottom pilons on either side." Markers highlighted the areas Al was describing.

"Those look like rocket launchers," Liam said. "Although much bigger and more elegant."

"They are coherent light cannons. There are six cannons per side. They each fire two packets per second, which means twenty-four packets per second can be fired. How long you can maintain that rate of fire depends on the energy contained in each packet and what other systems are demanding energy from your power plant. Moving on to..."

"Wait," Liam interrupted. "I don't understand. What is coherent light and what is a packet?"

"Coherent light is what your scientists use to describe a laser beam. It is a beam of photons that have the same frequency. It does not dissipate. Incoherent light dissipates."

"So it is a laser beam," Liam said.

"No," Al disagreed. "The phased-array is closer

to what you call a laser beam. The cannon shoots packets of coherent light. Think of it as shooting a cannon ball. But instead of a lead ball, it is shooting a very condensed ball of coherent light."

"How does it do that? How do you form light into a ball?" Liam asked.

"I can explain the physics to you if you want."

"No, don't bother. I'm sure I would not understand it," Liam said, remembering Paul's comment that you just had to accept it sometimes. "So, what does this light cannon do?"

"The impact of a light packet with an object causes the packet to dissipate. The process is very fast and releases a lot of energy."

"It explodes," Liam translated.

"Precisely. Now, moving on. In addition to the shield generators, the pilons also carry sensor arrays. There are both active and passive sensors that provide 360-degree coverage in a variety of bandwidths. We will discuss these later as well. But for now, I am merely giving you an overview. Let's move to the cockpit." A cut-away image of the cockpit appeared in the air. Your fighter is a two-seater, you will be flying with Paul."

A surge of disappointment flowed through Liam. He would not be able to fly. Paul would since he already demonstrated that he was an excellent pilot. Liam tried to force down the disappointment. "Are all the other fighters single-seaters?" Liam asked.

"Yes," Al answered. "You will be flying this one so Paul can handle tactical."

"I will be flying it?"

"Of course," Al said. "Combat flying and running tactical would be too distracting for one person. Now can we get back to the cockpit controls?" Al asked.

"Sure," Liam said, somehow suppressing his whoop for joy that he would be flying the fighter. Liam stared at the cockpit, trying to imagine sitting there flying the fighter. Something was wrong with it. Al was saying something, but he ignored it as he tried to figure it out. And then he spotted it. "What is with the seat?" Liam interrupted Al.

"The seat? Nothing is wrong with the seat," Al responded. "It is configured for human use. It is…" Al stopped. "Ahh, I have accessed your fighter plane schematics and now understand your question. This fighter does not have a traditional human airplane seat. Here you sit on top of the seat with your legs straddling it."

"Why?"

"There are control surfaces that you activate with your legs. But you are getting ahead of this presentation. We will discuss that…"

"… In much further detail later," Liam finished.

"You really are a very impatient student," Al said.

"I've heard that before," Liam agreed. And then tried to be quiet as Al continued the overview, explaining thrust, range, speed, and other aspects of the Delorian fighter.

# CHAPTER NINE

At noon the VR program wrapped up. Captain Paul was no longer in the room.

"Place the VR equipment back in their containers and seal them up," Lt. Turner instructed the group. When they had finished, Lt. Turner continued. "The problem with the VR training is that you will all get fat and lazy sitting in these comfy seats all day. We can't have that, particularly you Marines. So, you have fifteen minutes to change into PT clothes and meet me out in the hangar. After PT we will serve lunch."

"More MRE's?" someone from the back asked.

"For now, yes," Lt. Turner answered, eliciting several moans from the group. "Fifteen minutes, folks. Dismissed."

Fifteen minutes later they reassembled and after doing the usual pushups and sit-ups, headed out for a couple laps around the airfield. Lt. Turner led the group. When they finished, they were told they had two hours to shower and eat before reporting back to the classroom. The MRE's were in the same place as before. As it was a nice day, most of the trainees took their MRE's out the back door of the hangar, to a grassy field as it beat eating on the hangar floor or out on the tarmac.

They fell into groups and made introductions, since until now they really hadn't had a chance to meet their fellow classmates. Those that already knew each other,tended to group together.

"What do you make of all this?" Sarah Tenneson asked. A Navy Ensign, she had been training in helicopters at Whiting Field outside Pensacola when Captain Paul had selected her. A red head, she had the personality to match.

"A little cloak and daggery, don't you think?" Brenda Donaldson, one of her fellow flight students at Whiting replied.

"I thought black ops would be more realistic. Right now, all we are doing is playing computer games," Chuck Williams complained. At five foot, five, he was near the bottom of the old height requirements for pilots. He compensated by being aggressive, sporting a severe crew cut and spending as much time as he could at the weights. "I'm wondering if I made a mistake joining this group," he said. "I gave up jets for this. It does not look like we are saving the world."

"Not unless we are going to be invaded by Space Invaders," Carlos Santiago said with a laugh, trying to lighten the mood. Carlos was an easy-going Lieutenant with the Coast Guard in Mobile, transitioning to the Jayhawk helicopter for Search and Rescue. He had big brown eyes and a wide smile that made him a favorite with the ladies. Unlike the stereotypical aviator, he was rather shy, which made him even more popular.

"Yea," Alex Graham, another helicopter pilot said. "The only thing missing from the VR was the background music."

"Yes, but the tech is crazy advanced," Phillip Arnold said. "I've played with VR before and this stuff is way past it. Not a glitch in the program."

"What do you think about this A.I. nonsense?" Patrick Tanaka asked. "Come on. Sentient? Really? Who are they trying to fool?"

"Mine was pretty good," Jeffrey Shea said. "It felt like I was talking to a human, not a computer program. It was that smooth."

"Maybe it is a human we are talking to," Teddy Watson said. "Maybe they are trying to trick us."

"Why would they do that?" Katie Jerguson replied.

"What do you make of this Captain Paul guy?" Karen Dodson interjected. "He looks like a civilian."

"If he is, I bet he has some real pull," Alex said.

The conversations ran back and forth as the

trainees tried to figure out what was going on. Finally, their time was up and they stowed their trash and reported back to the classroom.

Lt. Turner informed them they would have two and a half more hours with the VR and then they would break for supper, MRE's again, and some personal time and then meet back in the classroom for one last session at 1900 hours. "Tonight's session will dispel any doubts you might be having about joining this program," Lt. Turner added.

With that, they donned the VR equipment. When the system came on, they found themselves in a standard ready room with Lt. Turner standing on a raised platform at the front of the room.

"Welcome back," Lt. Turner said. "Our enemy this afternoon is once again the dreaded Space Invader," he said, turning to a screen behind him that showed the space invader fleet heading down the screen. A few groans came from the audience. "However, this time we will be running tactics. The flight controls will be the same as this morning; basic stick, throttle, foot pedals. Your A.I. will notify you if you have to worry about anything else, like fuel or battle damage. You will be paired off in groups of two, three, and more, depending on how you progress. This program will not be static. It will be the best video game you have ever played."

"Now the purpose of this program," Lt. Turner continued. "is not to get used to the flight controls.

They are nothing like what you will be using later. Rather, the purpose is to get you thinking in three dimensions in a combat setting. We are picking space as there is no up or down. We want to see how quickly you can adapt to three dimensions, with a wingman or squad and while in combat. We are using our dreaded Space Invaders as we did not want to make this too realistic and scare you to death while trying to adapt. That will come later."

"Any questions?"

"What are the mission parameters?" Chuck Williams asked.

"Your A.I. will provide them to you at the start of each iteration, along with your assets and teammates. Ok. Now to your fighters. And may the force be with you," Lt. Turner added with a chuckle.

"You are mixing up your movie themes," Carlos said, but found himself alone in a cockpit as he finished his sentence.

"Lt. Turner seems fond of Star Wars," Carlos' A.I. answered. "Many of his comments can be traced to that movie series."

"So, what is our mission, Mr. A.I.," Carlos asked after recovering from the sudden switch of scenes.

"You are lead. Lt. Williams is your wingman. His call sign is Green Two. You are Green One. Here is the battle space." A hologram appeared in front of Carlos. "Here is the enemy," the A.I. continued as a circle showed in the hologram around a group of fighters. "Best estimate is ten enemy fighters. These are asteroids." More circles. "Don't let them hit you. Mission is simple. Attack and destroy the enemy fighters without getting hit by the asteroids or shot down by the enemy. Questions?"

"No, I guess not." No sooner had he spoken than he was hurtling towards the enemy ships, coming at them from the side and high, about ten-o'clock. "Woah, that was fast," Carlos said as he grabbed the stick. He wiggled it and the ship wiggled in response. "Green Two, do you copy?"

"Roger, Green One," came the immediate response.

Carlos thought fast. "Green Two. I guess we will go straight in at this angle, hit the middle of their formation and then bank right behind them and come up their tails. You good with that?"

"Roger."

"Let's see how fast these things will go," Carlos said as he pushed the throttle forward.

"This display shows where you and your wingman are in relation to the enemy," the A.I. said, lighting up a head's up display on the cockpit's screen.

They shot down in tandem and hit the center of the enemy formation. Carlos' twin tracers tore into the first ship, which exploded in a very satisfactory manner. He switched targets to a second ship and then a third as he shot past, noting that each exploded. He saw a couple other explosions out of the corner of his eye and figured his wingman had gotten them. Checking quickly to see where his wingman was, he banked to the right and did a three-sixty to come up behind the enemy formation. This was going to be easy.

As he lined up to shoot the next ship, the five remaining enemy fighters split off in five different directions. He lagged a second and then veered off after the nearest fighter, noting that his wingman was staying on his six. The enemy fighter zigged and zagged as he tried to put the crosshairs on it. He shot twice and missed. He shot again and clipped the fighter, sending some debris flying off into space. He lined up again and finally got off a clean shot and the fighter exploded.

"Yah!" he yelled, as he made the kill. And then his fighter shuddered and went into a spin, followed by a flash of white.

"I am afraid that you have died," his A.I. said. "As did your wingman."

"What? How?"

Both he and his wingman were sitting side by side back in the ready room, with a virtual flight instructor standing in the front. "Welcome to the afterlife," the flight instructor was saying.

"Someone has a sense of humor," Carlos whispered.

"Here is why you got killed," the instructor continued. A hologram appeared next to him as he continued to narrate. "Your initial approach was fine. The enemy in this simulation was sleeping and you hit them unawares. That will not happen in real life. When you turned and approached from the rear they scattered and when you fixated on this fighter, the others came up your tail and lit you up." He paused as they watched the hologram battle.

"Situational awareness, gentlemen. How often have you heard that? You have to watch everywhere at once, even during a dogfight. Or more accurately, especially in a dogfight. Now let's try it again, and this time try not to get killed."

They were back in their fighters. This time as they approached the enemy formation, the enemy saw them coming and scattered before they got off a shot. The rest of the short simulation they were fighting for their lives, trying to avoid getting shot down by ten enemy fighters. They lasted forty-two seconds.

They died in the third, fourth and fifth simulations as well, without killing a single enemy. When they were killed the last time, they found themselves back in the ready room with all the other trainees. Everyone looked exhausted. The flight instructor was not on the stage, so the trainees started talking.

"Did anyone not get killed?" someone asked.

"I got killed every time," Teddy responded.

"Me too," someone from the back said.

"I don't know what we are learning from this?" someone else complained. "We're not fighting space invaders."

"You are learning spatial awareness," Lt. Turner said from the front stage. The trainees quieted down. "And yes, you all died, "Lt. Turner continued. "But your scores actually improved tremendously as the exercise progressed. Your A.I.'s intentionally kept increasing the complexity of the simulation so you would have to push yourselves. It is okay to die in these simulations. It will keep us from getting killed later."

"We will be ending the simulation shortly," he continued. "When we do, you will be free to shower, relax, have dinner — yes, MRE's — although hopefully not too much longer. And then meet back here at 1900 hours. Captain Paul will brief you tonight on what you can expect in this operation."

"Between now and the 1900 hour meeting you all get to have physicals. When the VR ends, five of you stay in the classroom. We will then rotate five at a time until we are done. Any questions?"

When there were no questions, the simulation ended and the trainees found themselves sitting in their chairs in the classroom. They put away their VR equipment and headed next door to their barracks.

Five trainees stayed back in the classroom, Teddy Watson, Carlos, Alex Graham, Donna Peterson and Katie Jerguson. Lt. Turner turned to the group. "Follow me," He stepped off stage and headed to a previously unused door at the side of the classroom. The five followed and found themselves in room about the same size as the classroom. Folding tables were stacked against the far wall along with cardboard boxes marked, 'folding chairs.' In the center of the room were two folding tables, a laptop computer and a storage box not bigger than the laptop. Liam sat in the only chair. Next to the tables was a tall clear tube that reached the ceiling and was about four feet in diameter. One side was open.

"You're kidding, Teddy said, "you have an airport scanner here?"

"It looks like one," Lt. Turner conceded. "But it is a medical grade scanner. Now take off all your clothes and pile them on that table," Lt. Turner instructed as he sat in the chair and opened the laptop. The trainees looked at each other.

"Come on, don't be shy," Lt. Turner said. "You're in the military. You think there is any privacy?"

"Hey, I'm not shy," Chuck said, pointedly looking at Katie as he took off his flight suit.

Katie hit him on the shoulder. "I'm sure there is nothing there I want to see. So keep your eyes to yourself."

The group reluctantly took off their clothes, studiously avoiding looking at each other after that exchange. "Alex, you're first. Step into the scanner."

Alex eyed the scanner as he placed his clothes on the table. "Dog tags, too," Lt. Turner said as Alex was about to step into the scanner.

Carlos laughed. "He doesn't mind taking off his clothes, but he doesn't want to take off his dog tags."

"Hey, these are government issued," Alex replied as he pulled his dog tags over his head and dropped them on his pile of clothes.

"Put your feet on the marks," Lt. Turner said.

Alex looked down. Two footprints were drawn on the floor. "You sure this isn't an airport scanner?"

Lt. Turner ignored the comment. "Stand straight, arms slightly away from your side with your palms facing forward."

Alex straightened up and noticed a decal on the glass in front of him with a diagram of a person standing as Lt. Turner had instructed. "Now state your full name and rank."

"Graham, Alex J., Lieutenant, Junior Grade, United States Navy," Alex said.

There was a soft hum and then, just like an

airport scanner, a four-inch-wide panel the height of the tube started to slowly spin around him. It glowed with a soft blue light. The panel moved around him six times in about fifteen seconds, slowly changing from blue to green to orange as it did.

"Beam me up, Scotty," Teddy said. The others laughed.

When the bar stopped moving, two handprints glowed white in the glass in front of Alex.

"Put your hands against the handprints," Lt. Turner said.

Alex complied and the light turned red and the glass seemed to warm up. After ten seconds the light turned off.

"You can step out," Lt. Turner said.

"That is straight out of Star Trek."

"It is pretty high tech," Lt. Turner agreed. "Now I have to give you a vaccine and you are on your way."

Alex glanced at Lt. Turner, looking for a needle. Instead, Lt. Turner picked up a circular patch from the box on the table and stepped over to Alex, holding the patch up. "This will be the easiest shot you ever receive," Lt. Turner said. "I am going to place this patch on the side of your neck. It will administer the vaccine. No needle. No pain. You might feel a little warmth for a second or two. That's it."

Alex eyed the patch suspiciously, but stood while Lt. Turner placed it on the side of his neck. There was a moment of warmth and then Lt. Turner took off the patch and tossed it on the table. "That's it. You can get dressed. Go back to the barracks and send another person in."

"That's it?" Alex asked. "That was a physical?"

"Pretty neat," Lt. Turner said. "No poking or prodding."

"Too bad," Chuck said, "he was hoping for poking and prodding."

"Jeez, why don't you grow up," Katie complained. "Choose him next so we can get him out of here," she added, turning to Lt. Turner.

"You heard the lady," Lt. Turner said to Chuck. "You know the drill, step in." Chuck strutted into the scanner.

"Lord, he's strutting like a rooster," Katie said.

"I can't see why," Donna deadpanned. The others laughed.

Lt. Turner repeated the process until all the trainees had been scanned and the information was uploaded to the Delorian's web. Paul had told him this would help the Delorians sync the pilots with the fighter's tech. When Lt. Turner finished the last physical, he glanced at his watch. He had just enough time to grab some food and shower, before he had to prepare for the 1900 meeting.

# CHAPTER TEN

After the physical, Karen Dodson grabbed a packet of MRE's and went out the front to get some fresh air. She walked to the edge of the hangar and sat down with her back to the wall and tore open the MRE packet. As she was rummaging through the packet, Donna Peterson wandered over.

"Mind if I join you," Donna asked. When Karen nodded, she sat down next to her. "They are not much for privacy around here," Donna said as she tore open her MRE.

"No, they are not," Karen agreed. "Although with most of these guys, I really don't mind. They are being gentlemen. Except that Chuck Williams guy. The way he stares just makes my skin crawl."

"Yea," Donna agreed. "I think he made everyone feel uncomfortable."

They sat in silence while they ate their MRE's.

"This is the oddest program I have ever been in," Karen broke the silence. "The VR tech is amazing, but why play Space Invaders with it?"

"And what is with this run-down hangar?" Donna added. "I know he said 'Black Ops,' but Hurlburt runs black ops missions and it is not in the middle of nowhere. I don't get it."

"Hopefully, this Captain Paul will explain it tonight," Karen said.

After another meal of MRE's, the trainees met in the classroom at 1900 hours for the last briefing of the day. Lt. Turner was standing in front of the class. After calling for silence, he turned to the large screen in the front of the room and tapped something on his wrist.

Captain Paul appeared on the screen, the view from his shoulders up. He wore a black, skin-tight suit. The rest of the background was dark and indistinct.

"Lunar One to Base, do you copy?" Captain Paul said.

"Five-by-five, Lunar One," Lt. Turner answered.

"Good," Captain Paul continued. "Ladies and Gentlemen, this is a laser carried encrypted transmission, so I can be freer than I normally would be on the air. I am about to provide you with a demonstration. This is your second test. To determine whether you can accept what you are about to see and adapt to the new reality it will provide." Captain Paul let his comments sink in.

"I am flying sixty kilometers above you, or at 316,800 feet. That is the Karman line for those of you who read aerospace statistics, the line demarcating the start of space. I am not flying the fighter I promised you, that will come later. Rather I am merely flying a small transport. I call it a shuttle. However, this shuttle's capabilities are far beyond anything any of you have flown, or even seen. My demonstration will be brief because of security concerns. However, I will take some risks as I think it will be necessary to convince you of what I am about to tell you." With that, Captain Paul pulled a black visor over his head and face. "Lt. Turner," Captain Paul continued, "would you escort everyone outside."

Lt. Turner escorted everyone out of the building onto the edge of the airstrip where they had a clear view of the night sky.

Lt. Turner spoke into the device on his wrist before turning to the group. "All right everyone, focus your attention to the area of the sky over here," he pointed, "to the right of Orion's belt." It was a moonless night and the stars were easy to see. Soon, everyone noticed that one of the stars was slowly moving across the sky. It gained speed, changed direction by forty-five degrees before suddenly crossing the horizon like a shooting star before it disappeared. Then nothing.

A murmuring of voices could be heard as the seconds stretched out. "Is that it?" someone asked skeptically. "Give him a couple of minutes to get down here," Lt. Turner said, "he was pretty high."

"He couldn't have been that high," one of the pilots objected. "A U-2 could only go about 70,000 feet."

"Unless he is in SpaceX," another said.

"I don't think SpaceX was due to launch anytime soon," another objected.

The arguments continued until suddenly the ground shook as a sonic boom hit them, causing most of them to jump. One pilot laughed. "Oh boy, he is going to get into trouble for that one."

"Didn't you get your butt chewed for doing that, Jeffrey?" someone else asked.

"Don't want to talk about it," Jeffrey replied. Jeffrey Shea, an Air Force Captain, had been called in front of command for breaking the sound barrier over a residential area during a training flight in a T-38 Talon. The continuing repercussions were one of the reasons he had agreed to join Captain Paul's program.

"All right everyone," Lt. Turner yelled to the group. "Double-time it back through the hangar and out into the field in the back."

"Don't we get to watch him land?" someone objected.

"He is landing in the field, not out here in the open," Lt. Turner explained. "Now double-time." With that, he ran back to the hangar. In under a minute everyone was out on the field behind the hangar. It was the size of a football field, with tall pine trees surrounding it on three sides and the hangar on the fourth.

"He's landing here?" someone asked.

"Must be VTOL," another responded.

"Going to kick up hell of a lot of dust," another said, looking around. "Shouldn't we be under cover?"

"We're fine here," Lt. Turner responded. "Watch over the trees to the south," he added. "He's coming in now."

A dark shape materialized above the trees at the far side of the field. It did not have any running lights and the only way to make it out was where it blocked out the background stars. It moved slowly over to the center of the field and then hovered about two-hundred feet in the air before gradually coming down. At first there was no sound, then only the faintest, almost musical hum. As the craft descended below treetop level the floodlights on the outside of the hangar came on, bathing the field in light.

The craft was sleek, all rounded edges and flowing curves. It was triangular, with the larger end near the back, roughly fifteen feet long, five feet high and seven wide. The surface appeared smooth. It was dark blue, almost black, which made it hard to distinguish as it seemed to soak up the light. A smooth spoiler ran about one foot over the back of the craft. Four landing struts extended from the craft as it landed silently on the field not twenty feet from the watching crowd.

A moment later a door in the side of the craft near the front slid up into the roof, revealing a person sitting inside dressed all in black, head covered with a featureless black helmet. The pilot climbed out of the craft and faced the crowd. The helmet retracted revealing Captain Paul. A murmur of voices arose.

Captain Paul held up his hand for silence. "This," Captain Paul said, pointing to the craft for emphasis, "is a spaceship." He let the word hang. "At least that is what you would call it. I call it a shuttle as it has limited range. It can go to the Moon, as Lt. Turner can attest. However, real spaceships go much farther." Captain Paul paused again to let his words sink in.

"I will give you ten minutes to look over the shuttle. The controls are locked, but be careful touching the skin, it might still be hot after the reentry you witnessed. Then I will answer questions. After that, you will each get a twenty-minute flight in the shuttle. It only sits four so it will take two and a half hours to complete the entire group. That is all we will do tonight. Tomorrow you will start simulator training for the fighters. You will have the rest of the night to get a grip on what I am about to tell you, because I need your head in the game tomorrow."

Paul and Liam stood off to the side and watched

as the pilots examined the shuttle.

"You think they will believe you?" Liam asked Paul.

"If not, then we will have to ask Sally to make a cameo appearance," Paul said.

"Live?" Liam asked.

"Yes, we would have to. After the VR, they won't trust anything on video. I wouldn't," Paul said.

"That's why you got them all inoculated," Liam said, remembering his visit with Sally.

"Yes. Although we had to do that before we move to Lunar Base. There will be Delorian support staff there."

"I still can't believe we have a base on the moon."

"We don't yet," Paul replied. "The Delorians are building it as we speak. Fortunately, they can construct it rather quickly."

"And it's on the dark side so we can't see it from Earth?" Liam asked.

"Exactly."

A few minutes later Paul walked up to the pilot door of the shuttle and turned to the group. "Form a semicircle on me and sit down." They sat in three semicircles and looked up at Paul.

"What I am about to tell you will keep you up all night," Paul started. "If you haven't figured it out already, this is alien technology. This is not something we created. We can't even get close. Right now we can barely get off planet and each launch is a massive undertaking. Tonight, this shuttle will go from here to the edge of space eight times before midnight. And it will be piloted by Al, who is an A.I. Tonight you will see first-hand some of the capabilities of an A.I."

Paul looked around the group, trying to gauge their reactions. "And yes," Paul continued. "Aliens are real. Aliens are living here on Earth, hidden, and in our solar system. I call these aliens, Delorians. And no, I am not referring to the car in *Back to the Future*. Delorian is the closest I can get to pronouncing what they call themselves. This is their tech and they have given it to us. They have modified the controls so we can operate it. And yes, they are friendly."

"That is the good news," Paul said as he looked out over the group, trying to gauge their reactions. "The bad news is there are other aliens out there that are not friendly. One group of these not-friendly aliens is planning on attacking Earth. Right now, they are massing at a portal that will drop them into our solar system. The Delorians are preparing to defend Earth. We will be the rearguard to defend against any that get past the Delorians. That is our mission and that is what we will be training for."

Paul paused and looked out at the group. There was stunned silence.

"Sir," trainee Erickson interrupted the long silence. "With due respect, why should we believe you?"

"Don't," Paul answered. "Not without proof. And the proof is here," Paul said, patting the shuttle. "Do we have anything even remotely close to this? You are all pilots. You know the forces required to move platforms here on Earth." Paul took a step away from the shuttle. "Al, take her up ten feet and hover." The shuttle suddenly rose and hovered ten feet off the ground, a slight hum the only sound. "Can we do this?" Paul asked again.

"And in a few minutes, you will be flown to the edge of space. When you come back, you can ask your question again."

"Yes, Trainee Jerguson," Paul said, pointing to another pilot.

"Are we going to meet these aliens?"

"Yes. Although not tonight. I thought I would break things to you one step at a time."

"How are we going to fight these other aliens?" another trainee asked.

"I will go over the strategy and tactics tomorrow," Paul said. "Right now, I think it is enough that you have to accept that we are not alone and that you will be defending Earth. I think that is enough for one night."

"Who else knows about the aliens?"

"Not many," Paul said. "There are only a handful. Although the numbers have significantly increased now that a war is coming. Four squadrons of fighters are being trained."

"Why aren't more people in the loop?" someone asked.

"We'll discuss that tomorrow when we discuss strategy and tactics."

"How do we know we can trust them?"

"Ah, the age-old question," Paul said. "We are after all a very suspicious race. Well, one answer is because they just gave us their tech. You will see the broader picture tomorrow." A number of other hands went up.

"As frustrating as this will be, I will stop the questions now or we will never get the shuttle flights going. You need to see the capability of this craft to believe what I am telling you. After that you will probably be more likely to believe what I am telling you. So, let's take this one step at a time. We need to get the shuttle flights going so I for one can get a good night sleep tonight, even if you won't."

"Get with Lt. Turner," Paul continued. "He has spacesuits for you. They are just like this one," he said, pointing to the black skin-tight suit he was wearing. "It's one size fits all. Lt. Turner will explain it. One important thing, you have to strip naked before you put on the suit. That includes dog tags. Do not wear them under these suits. Now let's get going so I can get home tonight at a reasonable hour."

With that the trainees turned to Lt. Turner to get outfitted for their flight.

# CHAPTER ELEVEN

The next day at 0800, Captain Paul was sitting in the front of the classroom when the trainees filtered in. Rather than a suit, he was wearing a dark blue polo shirt with khaki pants, along with a pair of topsiders. Although the trainees had done PT and had another breakfast of MRE's, they still did not look well rested. They were surprised to find a large coffee pot sitting on a table in the corner, the smell of fresh coffee filling the room. They quickly hurried over to it and pulled cups from a nearby stack. Only then did they move to their chairs.

"Did any of you get any sleep last night?" Captain Paul asked as the trainees were moving towards their chairs. A few of the trainees shook their heads, most looked beat. "It took me a little while to get used to the whole alien idea when I first found out," Captain Paul admitted. When all the trainees had their coffee and were seated, he continued. "You will be glad to know that through this door to my left," he pointed, "there is a break room. It is currently being set up, so soon you should be able to have your meals in there. And rather than MRE's, you will have a selection of food from an automated menu that should be superior to MRE's."

"Anything is superior to MRE's," someone muttered in the back.

"Now, let's turn to your training," Captain Paul continued. "First, an overview of our mission. The Delorians have a base near Jupiter. There is a portal past Jupiter which allows access to our solar system. I am not going to pretend to understand the physics. I think of it as a wormhole. Although I don't know if technically that is accurate. But that is where the access to our system is. The Delorians will engage the invaders at the portal."

"There are several possible scenarios. For our purposes, I'm going to call the enemy 'Red Force.' The Delorians told me their name, but it is unpronounceable. One scenario is that the Delorians defeat Red Force at the portal and we are never called into play. Under that scenario, the people of Earth may never even know about the battle. It will all depend on where our telescopes are facing at the time and how much energy is expended in the battle.

"More importantly, as Jupiter will be between thirty-five and forty-three light minutes from Earth, depending on the time of year of the attack, we will have a communications lag. Since Delorian communications travel at light speed, we might not know about the attack for up to forty-three minutes.

"A second scenario is Red Force splits their forces so some engage the Delorians, while another portion slips past for an attack on Earth. Under this scenario, we will have no warning before the attack. We will have to defend Earth. Our tactics will depend upon whether we are facing fighters, or if some of the support ships make it past the Delorians. We will run simulations for several different events. Think of Red Force as a space faring version of one of our Navy carrier battle groups. We know they will have an aircraft carrier carrying their fighters. They will also have several support ships. What we won't know until they get here, is what type of support ships will they bring? Destroyers? The space version of an amphibious landing craft? Troop carriers? Missile launchers? A lot will determine on what their intentions are for Earth. I will get back to this in a minute.

"A third scenario is that Red Force defeats the Delorians and attacks Earth with their capital ships intact. If that occurs, we will be wiped out in minutes. So, we will have to count on the Delorians to prevent that from happening."

"A pleasant thought," Patrick Tanaka whispered to the trainee sitting next to him.

"Now back to the second scenario," Captain

Paul continued. "The Delorians have informed me there are a couple different attacks we can expect, depending on what Red Force wants to accomplish. The worst case," Paul paused. "Actually, they are all bad cases. But the worst case is that they want our planet. They want Earth for themselves and humanity gone. In that case they just have to seed our atmosphere with a biological agent to wipe us out. That means that if just one ship, or one missile with the right payload, gets through, everyone dies. They could drop a highly contagious, lethal airborne virus, and just wait for us to die out. It would make the Covid pandemic of 2020 look like a case of the sniffles.

"Fortunately, the Delorians don't believe Red Force has that capability. Red Force would have to have been here and studied us long enough to create the virus. Although there have been incursions by Red Force already," Paul glanced over at Liam, "the Delorians don't think the incursions have been sufficient for Red Force to conduct sufficient studies to make such an agent."

"That means the alien abduction wackos were telling the truth?" Chuck whispered to Phillip.

Captain Paul ignored the whispered comments. "Another possibility is that Red Force wants our resources. Under that scenario, they would come down and blast us to bits until we were not a threat to their mining operations. Our population would be insignificant to them. Or, they would blast us to bits and then use the remaining population as slave labor to conduct their mining operations. This is the scenario the Delorians think is most likely.

"The good news is that under this scenario, if a few fighters slip by us, it does not mean the end of the world. Or at least the end of the world as we know it."

"Any questions so far?"

There was silence in the room. Finally, a hand went up.

"Trainee Graham."

"If some of the, uh, Red Force gets through. How are we going to stop them? There's only thirty-two of us. I'm assuming this task force of theirs will be pretty large. After all, they are attacking a planet."

"Fair question. We should be able to field thirty-one fighters in our squadron. The fighters are single-seaters. We will fly ten flights of three fighters each, with one command fighter. Our tactics will depend upon how many get through. There are three other squadrons like ours currently in training. Depending on the situation, we may fight alone, or we may combine with the other squadrons. Only time will tell. But for our current training purposes, we will assume the other squadrons are tied up elsewhere and we are on our own.

"To address the second part of your question. One of our strategic assumptions, or force multipliers to use a term the military loves, is that any Red Force that gets past the Delorians will think Earth is easy pickings. They do not know about us and they think there is nothing on Earth that can touch them."

"But we have nukes," someone blurted out from the back.

"Yes, but no delivery system to hit them with," Captain Paul responded. "They can drop out of space at will and attack our bases, our infrastructure, power, dams, roads, and then fly back into space before we could respond. You saw how fast my shuttle is. We don't have anything that can touch that shuttle. And a shuttle is no match for a fighter. So, all they have to do is hit us quickly enough that our society collapses. No electricity, no food, no water. How long could we last? How long would we keep our planes flying? And in a dogfight, our planes would be horribly mismatched. No, they believe that the Delorians are their only threat. That is our advantage." Captain Paul said. "Any other questions?"

"Do we know when they are coming?"

"Not for at least six months."

"Six months!" someone said in surprise. There was an accompanying murmur.

"They are massing at the entrance to the portal.

The Delorians say it will take them at least six months to get their ships in position. The longer they take after six months means the more ships they attack us with. So, we have to hope they attack in six months."

"Earth will be attacked in six months and we are only now preparing for it?" Chuck Williams asked.

"The Delorians only learned of this threat recently, which is why we only have four squadrons in training right now. Until now, their plan was non-involvement. They wanted us to evolve on our own without their interference. Which until now made sense. Can you imagine what we, and I mean humanity, would do if we discovered there were aliens out there? And if we got hold of any of their technology? We would probably wipe ourselves out."

"But they are giving us the tech now."

"Yes and no. We are a black ops operation. No one outside of this room and the other three squadrons knows about our tech and no one will, at least until the fighting starts. After that, all bets are off."

"But shouldn't we mass produce it?"

"We don't have the technology to produce any of this now. It would take years to retool and train to produce any of this. No, we are on our own for now."

"And we are not going to warn anyone?"

"Have any of you been involved in the wargaming that the military does? Not Reforger or Bright Star, I mean the paper wargames?"

Everyone shook their heads 'no.'

"The military has done this for years," Captain Paul explained. "Engaged in paper war games covering a multitude of scenarios. Commanders of small units all the way up to Generals are given a scenario and have to respond to it with real life solutions. They run the scenario through S-1, 2, 3, everyone, until they have the best possible solution. Then they write up an after-action report and file it away. The theory is that if something happened, they could pull out the file with the real-life answer and implement it, without having to reinvent the wheel. And these plans are updated every so often so they remain current.

"There is a plan that covers this attack. No one realizes it is a real possibility. It is called 'Plan X.' It was a mandatory war game that everyone probably hated because it seemed so unreal. The premise was that the U.S. was attacked and infrastructure knocked out. It did not mention aliens. The question was how would the military respond. All the bases were involved. Most of the response is geared to containing civil unrest and trying to supply food, water, medicine to the population. For the fighter wings, there are secret orders on how to defend against an alien threat. These orders are sealed. No one has seen them. They will be opened only if Plan X is implemented."

"That will be a hell of a surprise when they open them," Carlos deadpanned.

"Once they arrive in our solar system, how long will it take to get to Earth? Jupiter is a long way away," Teresa asked.

"It is," Captain Paul agreed. "However, their big ships have jump capability. The way the Delorians explain it is that you need a portal to get from one system to another. But inside a system a ship can jump from point to point in seconds. That is the danger. Once you get trained and we are at our base, we will have to be ready to scramble at a moment's notice."

"I will take more questions later," Captain Paul said. "We have to start training. But before we hook up the VR, I want to show you these video clips."

Captain Paul signaled Lt. Turner to turn on the video. Stars filled the screen behind him. "This view is taken from the shuttle camera," Captain Paul said as he stepped to the side. "The same shuttle you flew in last night. We shot this video two days ago. Lt. Turner is piloting the shuttle, by the way."

The trainees watched the stars on the screen. A shape shot past, too fast to make out what it was. It stopped in the distance and the shuttle caught up. It was a Delorian fighter, dubbed the X-wing by Lt. Turner. It stayed on the screen for a few seconds and then shot forward again, almost out of sight. Once again it slowed until it maintained its pace about a quarter-mile away.

"This is what you are used to doing," Captain Paul narrated as the fighter banked left and right and then up and down, all while maintaining its relative position in front of the shuttle. "And this is just some of what the fighter can do," Captain Paul continued. Without warning the fighter dropped straight down, while still staying in front of the shuttle. Then it shot laterally to the right, its nose still pointing forward. It rolled, shot straight up, came back to center, spun in circles in place, then suddenly was just a few feet from the shuttle's front window, facing the shuttle, while flying backwards. A couple trainees in the crowd jumped. "Bang, you're dead," Captain Paul said.

"Let me show you this clip," Captain Paul said. "Just in case the first was not sufficiently interesting for you. This one is taken from the fighter." Paul signaled to Liam and the screen behind him showed a split screen. On the right side was a side view of a pilot and the fighter's control console. "I am piloting," Captain Paul said. The other half of the screen showed the forward view. At first, all you could see were stars. Then a shape materialized in the distance, which quickly turned into the shuttle. The stars moved back and forth as the fighter maneuvered until the view stopped with the shuttle head on, just a few feet in front of the fighter.

"The problem with space is that you don't have a perspective for speed and distances. This final clip will give you a better perspective." The view of the stars returned, then the stars shifted and the Moon appeared, centered in the distance. The view did not change, just the Moon in the center and the stars in the periphery. Captain Paul watched the assembled trainees closely. A minute passed and the view did not change. Two minutes. The trainees started getting restless, glancing around. Captain Paul waited. Three minutes. Four.

"Holy sh…" one of the trainees murmured. "The moon's getting bigger."

Suddenly they were all paying attention again as the moon was indeed getting larger on the screen. "This recording is not speeded up," Captain Paul broke the silence. The trainees watched, now mesmerized, as the Moon grew larger, until it filled the screen. The view of a single crater filled the screen before the fighter leveled off and flew just over the surface of the Moon. Craters rushed past, almost a blur. The fighter crossed the terminator into the dark side of the Moon, before finally banking and then slowing over a long crevasse on the moonscape. It followed the crevasse to its abrupt end in a large mound of dirt. A silver shape stuck out of the dirt half way up. The camera zoomed in, showing an open hatch and then panned across footprints leading to and away from the hatch. The video froze with the open hatch and footprints on the screen.

"Nine months ago, a Delorian ship was attacked and destroyed," Captain Paul told the assembled pilots. "The Delorian pilot managed to jettison in this escape pod, which crashed on the Moon. The pilot was rescued." "The footsteps you see are Lt. Turner's. He might share that story with you someday if you buy him a beer." Captain Paul paused for effect as the trainees stared at the screen and then Lt. Turner and then back again.

"Now put on your VR and your A.I.'s will introduce you to the fighter we will be flying.

# CHAPTER TWELVE

When the trainees turned on their VR, they found themselves standing out on a tarmac, with row upon row of Delorian fighters parked around them.

"Pay attention over here," a voice called out. They turned towards the voice and saw a man in a flight suit with Captain's bars standing next to one of the fighters. His hair was buzz cut and he looked like he had stepped out of central casting for a flight instructor scene.

"I already don't like this guy," Chuck Williams whispered to the trainee next to him. "He reminds me too much of my first flight instructor."

"This is a Delorian mid-range tactical fighter," the virtual flight instructor was saying. "It is not an X-wing, as your Lt. Turner likes to call it." That was a mistake as all of the pilots immediately saw it as an X-wing once the reference had been made.

"It's actually a lot cooler than an X-wing," Carlos whispered to Teddy, who was standing next to him. "Look how the wings sweep forward."

They listened as Captain Johnson spent the next couple hours going over the various characteristics of the craft. When the initial orientation session finally ended, the VR program discontinued and the trainees found themselves back in their chairs in the classroom. Lt. Turner was standing at the front of the room.

"You know the drill," Lt. Turner said. "On the tarmac ready for PT in fifteen minutes. Dismissed."

When the trainees had finished PT, showering and had another lunch of MRE's, they returned to the classroom only to have Lt. Turner tell them to fall out to the field behind the hangar, the one Captain Paul had landed the shuttle in the night before. There they found Captain Paul standing next to his gold Honda.

"How did he get his car here?" Chuck whispered. "Do you see any roads coming in here?"

"Makes you wonder where we are?" Katie said. "Can't be too far away if he is driving here."

Captain Paul motioned them to sit down, so they formed up in a semi-circle around him and sat in the grass. "I realize I am hitting you with a lot of new information and you probably still have some lingering doubts. So, I thought I would provide you with another little demonstration of this alien technology before you go back to the VR.

But, just to keep the suspense up a little longer, let me tell you the course plan for the next couple weeks."

"When you took your original flight training, you alternated through classroom work, looking at static displays and then simulators, before you got to fly. As you experienced first-hand this morning, the Delorians are very advanced with VR. Therefore, most of your preliminary class work will be done by interactive VR. I think you will find it is much more efficient. Also, just so you feel at home, we came up with CPT Johnson, the flight instructor you met this morning."

"I hate that guy," someone whispered loud enough to carry over the group. There was a round of chuckles.

"I thought you would get a kick out of him," Captain Paul said with a smile. "Although later when we break into private sessions, your A.I. will take over the training and you can lose CPT Johnson if you want. Or you can modify him into a better instructor. Your A.I. will tell you how to do that."

"Anyway, getting back to the training schedule. We will continue to do two main training sessions each day, morning and afternoon. If you want to study at any other time, you may come in and use your VR equipment. Your A.I. will come on line automatically and you can request to review anything you want. You can also request it in any format you want, including text books, lecture, hands on, or whatever works best for you. Being that the training is done VR with your private instructor, the training can be very versatile and individualized to fit your needs.

"We will be training VR for the next several weeks. How long we take depends on how quickly you progress. The first week will be introducing you to the fighter's controls. The actual fighters are single-seaters, although they can be configured as two-seaters. Your initial flight training will be in VR double-seaters, with you being the nav officer. First, you will familiarize yourself with the various non-flight controls of the fighter. The training modules will cover life support, navigation, the sensor suite, stealth properties, propulsion and armament. Once you have covered those topics, we will transition to learning how to fly the fighters. That is where things will get harder."

"Question?" Captain Paul said, pointing to Teddy Watson.

"Yes, Sir. How do you expect us to master all of this and learn how to fly in a combat setting in six months? Most of us have been training much longer than that and we haven't even progressed to our main aircraft."

"The practical answer," Captain Paul responded, "is that six months is the time we have so it will have to do. The realistic answer is that most activities, including some of the actual flying, will be done by your A.I. However, you have to know enough about the ship so you can instruct the A.I. on what configuration you want and be able to decide the best tactics. The A.I. can't fight the ship, but it can do a lot of the work for you. You also have to know the systems well enough so you can decide on trade-offs during combat. Do you want more stealth? Do you need more sensors? More power to the phased array? How do you juggle the power requirements and keep yourself alive and flying? You will learn to do these activities in tandem with your A.I."

Captain Paul pointed to another trainee who had raised her hand. "Why don't the Delorians just have the A.I.'s fight the ship? Why do they want us?"

"This is the same philosophical question that some of our scientists and military leaders are starting to grapple with right now," Captain Paul explained. "Do you want an autonomous fighting machine or not? The short answer is that the Delorians have decided not to allow a warship to be autonomous. They want a living, breathing entity to have the final say. Since I grew up on the Terminator movies and Skynet, I for one can understand their decision." Another chuckle went through the group.

"Anyway, you will need a very good working understanding of these fighters. The reason will become self-evident when we start to fly them. Which by the way, will be completely different than flying anything you have flown before."

"But I am getting ahead of myself," Captain Paul said. "Now for the demonstration. You will be seeing this in training. But I wanted to give you this demonstration before you went VR, so you knew this was real. First, I need a volunteer."

Several hands went up. "Trainee Avery," Captain Paul pointed to a young woman near the front of the group. "Would you be so kind as to take my car for a little spin?"

Avery looked at the Captain quizzically. "You do know how to drive a Honda?" Captain Paul asked. "It's got a push button start," Captain Paul continued. "And since it is a hybrid, it will be silent, at least at low speeds. I need three of you to climb in for the ride. The rest of you," Captain Paul said as Avery walked over and opened the car door, "Please stand back a little to give her some room."

Three trainees got in the car with Lt. Avery, while the rest stood up and took a few steps back. Avery closed the car door. "Can you hear me?" Captain Paul said, speaking into a device on his wrist that looked like a wide black band.

"Yes," came the response from the band.

"Good. Now take it around in a circle in the field. Nothing fancy. The trainees watched as the gold Honda drove around in a circle. They could see Lt. Avery through the window. She then drove back and stopped next to them and rolled down the driver's window. "How was it?" Captain Paul asked.

"Nice ride," Avery responded, a little confused. "It is very quiet."

"Do it again," Captain Paul said. "A little more aggressive this time and change the pattern, but don't race car it. And then come back here."

She drove around the field again, this time faster, throwing in some curves. She pulled up and stopped, looking at Captain Paul, obviously wondering what was going on.

"How was it?" Captain Paul asked.

"It's okay. "It's not a Corvette, but for a Honda Accord, it's fine," Avery responded with a smile.

"Gotcha," one of the trainees responded from the back.

Captain Paul smiled. "Oh, I think my Honda Accord can beat the pants off your Corvette," he said. "Put it in park and roll up the window and wait for my next command." She complied and watched Captain Paul through the driver's side window, her face showing her confusion. The three other trainees also looked confused.

"Al, reconfigure to shuttle," Captain Paul said. The trainees gasped as the Honda shimmered, metal flowing. Seconds later they were looking at the shuttle Captain Paul had flown the night before, but now it was the same color gold as the Honda. "Al, take it up twenty fleet and fly the same configuration as Avery's last drive." The shuttle flew Avery's course, staying twenty feet above the ground. "Al, bring her back down." Four struts extended and the shuttle landed gently.

Captain Paul glanced over at the trainees, who were all staring at the shuttle. "Al, stealth mode." The shuttle disappeared. The trainees stared at an empty field. "Al, open all four doors." The doors of the shuttle opened up into the ceiling. Now the inside of the shuttle was visible, but the outside was still invisible. "You can climb out now," Captain Paul said to the four shocked trainees in the shuttle. "And you can all go over and inspect the shuttle, just be careful you don't bang your shin against it. Although you can't see it, it is still there."

Captain Paul watched as the trainees moved around the shuttle, hands held out like blind men as they ran their hands over a metal body they could not see. After a few minutes, Paul said, "Al, stealth mode off," and the shuttle reappeared. "Now you know how I can go home every night for dinner," Captain Paul said to the group. "Commuting is really easy in this beauty." He turned to Avery. "Now do you believe that my Honda beats your Corvette?"

"Yes, Sir," she answered without hesitation.

"Lt. Turner," Captain Paul said.

"Yes, Sir."

"Shows over. Take the trainees back to the classroom. It's time to get back to work."

# CHAPTER THIRTEEN

The trainees filed back into the classroom. Brenda Donaldson sat in her recliner and put on the VR goggles. A First Lieutenant with the Air Force, she was currently assigned to Training Wing Five (TRAWING 5) at Naval Air Station, Whiting Field, for flight training on the Beechcraft T-6 Texan II turboprop, with aspirations of moving on to jets afterwards. She found flying came naturally for her and was intrigued by Captain Paul's promise of flying an advanced platform. She never expected that it meant flying alien technology and was still trying to comprehend what she had just seen during the latest demonstration.

She wondered if her A.I. was trying to develop a sense of humor when it started the VR program. "Welcome back, Brenda. This is the life support module, otherwise known as 'How do we keep you frail humans alive?' Unlike my core, which will be protected in the center of the fighter and does not have very specific requirements to stay alive, the human body is remarkably fragile."

As the A.I. reveled in the frailty of the human body, Brenda wondered if her A.I. was getting too funny. "In addition to the space skin you wore on the shuttle ride, you will have an outer spacesuit. It will not be as bulky as the NASA suits - I don't know how they move about in those - rather it will be more like a dry suit, if you are familiar with SCUBA diving. But not the real bulky dry suits, more form-fitting than those." The A.I. showed a holographic picture.

"These fighter's suits offer longer protection than the space skin and are more durable. They are still easy to move about in. However, if you are relying upon the suit to protect you, then things have gone very badly. The cockpit of the fighter is designed with full life support. You could actually fly in space without a suit, or anything at all."

"I don't think I will be flying a fighter naked, thank you," Brenda responded.

"Probably not," the A.I. agreed. "The cockpit life support controls are shown on these screens, although you probably will not deal with any of them as my job is to maintain proper life support. The cockpit usually will have air, typically with a 21% oxygen, 78% nitrogen mix. The cockpit will protect you from the radiation prevalent in space and temperature extremes. Your suit is a backup if your cockpit is compromised. Of course, if you are hit hard enough that your cockpit is compromised, you will probably be dead anyway."

"Please don't sugarcoat this presentation for me," Brenda said.

"Oh, sarcasm," A.I. said. "Well, it is still true. It would take a direct hit for the…"

"Can we just move on, rather than discussing all the ways I can die?"

"Okay. This is a mid-range fighter. It can stay out in space much longer than you can. There are hydration and nutrient dispensers in your suit that will keep you nourished. You can also urinate in the suit and it will be absorbed with no unpleasantries. I would not recommend defecating. That would be unpleasant."

"Thanks for the advice. How long do they anticipate these missions to last?"

"Mission parameters can range from several hours to several days."

"Several days? How do you not defecate for several days?"

"Before a mission of such length, all pilots should drink a cleansing solution that will clean out your digestive tract. After that, the waste from the nutrients in the suit will only pass as urine, so no problem."

"I really did not want to know that."

The A.I. went on to describe the location of the life support units, their capacity and how long they could regenerate from the ship, versus the much lower timeframe if only the spacesuit was utilized.

When the session ended, the trainees did their PT and, after showering and changing, headed into the hangar where the MRE's were stored. Brenda rummaged through the MRE's until she found one she could tolerate, meatballs in marinara sauce, and went out to the back field to sit in the grass and eat.

A few moments later, Donna Peterson came out and sat down with her. The two women could not be any more different in appearance. Where Brenda was a five foot, ten, big boned black woman, with closely cropped hair, Donna was barely five foot, five, blonde hair and blue-eyed. However, both of them had aggressive, no-nonsense personalities that served them well in their chosen profession.

"That was a sobering lesson," Brenda commented when Donna sat down. "I never realized how many ways you can die in space. Evidently my A.I. thinks it has a sense of humor and loves telling all the ways life support can fail."

"That is funny?" Donna asked.

"He thinks so."

"What else did he tell you?"

"You don't even want to know what prep we will have to do for extended missions," Brenda answered.

Before Brenda could expand on it, Katie Jerguson walked over and joined them. Katie had just finished initial flight training and was waiting for the next rotation of jet training to start when she had accepted Captain Paul's offer. A proud Texan, she kept her long brown hair in a pony tail that always threatened to come undone, in a very unmilitary manner. The ladies had naturally gravitated to each other, feeling a shared camaraderie in what was still a pretty male dominated profession.

"So what do you think of all this?" Katie asked as she ripped open her MRE.

"Which 'this' are you referring to?" Brenda asked. "This MRE, which is inedible? This, we are stuck in a hangar on a deserted airfield? Or, there are freaking aliens that are about to attack the Earth and we have to defend it?"

"Yes, this MRE is inedible," she said in disgust as she rummaged through the plastic MRE bag. "Yes, the freaking aliens. Do you believe this? If there are aliens, why aren't we mobilizing the entire military? Why are we training in some run-down hangar? None of this makes sense."

"Captain Paul explained that," Donna said.

"But can we believe him?" Katie asked. "About any of it?"

"Look at it the other way," Brenda replied.

"What motive does he have to lie? Why bring us out here? Its not like we are locked up. Granted we don't know where we are. But we all took survival training. We could hike out of here and find someone without too much trouble."

"But, aliens?" Katie asked again.

"How do you explain the tech?" Donna asked. "Forget the VR and the A.I., which is pretty impressive on its own. How do you explain his car? It turned into a spaceship and we all flew into space. Space! Tell me that this isn't alien tech!"

Katie sat in silence, staring at her uneaten MRE. "Then why not tell everyone about the aliens?"

"Oh, I agree with his reason for that one," Brenda said. "Can you imagine telling six billion people we are about to be attacked by aliens? First, no one would believe it without proof, and second, all the wackos would come out. It would be pandemonium."

"I just don't know," Katie said. "And if we are going to save the world, they need to feed us something other than MRE's."

* * *

Now that they knew what they were training for, the days became predictable. Wednesday was a repeat of Tuesday. PT, breakfast, then to the classroom for VR training. Lt. Turner promised the group that they would have a galley installed soon, so they would not have to eat MRE's much longer.

The VR presentations started with the trainees in the ready room, with Virtual CPT Johnson providing them an overview of the upcoming lesson. Then they would find themselves in the Delorian fighter receiving private instructions. Most trainees chose a private instructor other than the unpopular CPT Johnson. Some just had the A.I. provide the training, without giving it a virtual body.

"This is the sensor suite," the virtual Captain Johnson informed Chuck Williams. Chuck had decided to keep CPT Johnson, figuring that the gruff instructor would make him tougher. A holographic depiction of the fighter appeared, highlighting the ends of the four pilons where the sensors were located. "As you will recall from yesterday's briefing, the command console is dynamic, with various controls and interfaces present depending on what systems have been activated. When the sensor suite is chosen, the command console looks like this." Four screens in front of Chuck lit up. Captain Johnson proceeded to describe the screens and sensor controls.

"These screens are customizable. The default display is shown here. You have two types of sensors, active and passive. Active sensors send out a signal and then reads the return energy, much like a ping on a submarine sonar. Active sensors have greater range and sensitivity. The downside is that everyone knows where you are when you go active. You can minimize the risk by narrowing the band or angle of the 'ping,' but you cannot eliminate it. You can hide your location by bouncing the ping off another object before it is sent out, or sending it off a remote relay. That way the enemy will target the other object or the relay, rather than you.

"Passive sensors analyze signals already out there. You can receive them without giving away your position. Depending on conditions, their range and sensitivity vary greatly. All sensors can be avoided to some degree depending on the surrounding conditions and the technology being utilized. Even the stealth settings of the shuttle which Captain Paul demonstrated for you earlier, can be defeated by the right sensor sweep."

Captain Johnson described how each system would be utilized and how they could be controlled and their results interpreted on the command screens. The lesson ended with simulated flights, where the Chuck had to use the various sensors to locate potential threats.

When the session ended, the trainees ran PT, showered, changed, and with a lot of complaining, searched for a passable MRE packet. Most of them wondered out to the back field and sat in groups in the grass eating, enjoying getting out of the hangar on a clear sunny day.

"Thank heavens the A.I. will be running all of this," Carlos said to the group sitting around him.

"There is no way I can remember half of it, let alone control any of it. Maybe if I had a year or two, but in a day?"

"I thought flight school was tough, trying to learn the instrument panel," Daniel said. "This is a thousand times worse."

"I wonder why they are even bothering trying to teach us this? It's not like we will ever use it," Daniel added.

Lt. Turner was sitting on the grass nearby, silently eating. Although he joined the trainees for lunch, he typically did not talk much. However, at this last comment he decided to speak up. "What if you lose your A.I.?"

All heads turned his way.

"What? Sir," Carlos hastily added the Sir.

"What if you lose your A.I.?" Lt. Turner repeated.

"Is that possible? Wouldn't the ship be dead then, and you with it?" John asked.

"Several months ago, Captain Paul and I were coming back from a mission on the Moon," Lt. Turner began. "We were in the shuttle and a Red Force fighter started chasing us. We didn't know there was a threat back then. Captain Paul made a run for Earth's atmosphere while taking evasive maneuvers. We got hit several times. The shuttle has shields, but the enemy fire breached the shields and knocked out the A.I. Captain Paul had to fly the shuttle manually, or the shuttle's version of manual. You can't glide or auto-rotate a shuttle into the Earth's atmosphere. There was still some computing power in the shuttle, but it was very limited and Captain Paul had to get it back on line, while flying the shuttle and evading the fighter."

"So, what happened?" Carlos asked when Lt. Turner stopped. Some trainees sitting nearby had stopped talking and were listening as well.

"Damndest flying I have ever seen," Lt. Turner continued. "We were in a vicious spin. The inertial dampeners were down so we were pressed against our seats. The whole console had gone black. Somehow, Captain Paul managed to get two small screens up, one nav and one fire control. Yes, that shuttle is armed," Lt. Turner added when he saw the question on their faces.

"The fighter had much longer range than we did, but Captain Paul played dead as we spun into the atmosphere. He lured the fighter in close and right before it fired, he spun the shuttle around and blew the fighter out of the sky. To this day I can't tell you how he did it. He then accessed the propulsion system enough to manage a controlled crash that we both were able to walk away from. It was incredible. I tell you, the old man has forgotten more about these systems than any of us will ever learn." With that, Lt. Turner picked up his MRE and walked back into the hangar.

# CHAPTER FOURTEEN

Chuck flopped down on his bunk at 2200 Wednesday night, his mind rerunning the Delorian training. Somehow he fell asleep, only to wake up later that night. He eyed the clock next to his bunk. 2:35. He couldn't sleep. He was having trouble retaining the module training and felt the other trainees were way ahead of him.

Remembering that Captain Paul had said they could train with the VR anytime, he climbed out of his bunk, slipped on some shorts and quietly headed for the classroom. Although the classroom lights were dimmed, he had no trouble seeing as he made his way to his chair. He was about to sit down when he heard a thump. He stopped and listened. A few seconds later he heard another thump and a scraping sound. It appeared to come from the break room next door, the one they had done their physicals in. Looking over, he noticed light shining beneath the door.

Curious, he walked over and opened the door. The lights were on. The medical scanner was gone and now the room was set up with four rows of folding tables with chairs, much like a cafeteria. Across from him was a large gray cabinet that ran almost the length of the wall. Another noise came from behind the cabinet.

"Hey, who's there?" he called out as he threaded his way between the tables and chairs, heading for the back of the room. He was about at the end of the cabinet when he heard footsteps and a figure emerged from behind the cabinet. Chuck looked up and screamed. He jumped back and collided with some chairs and a table. Scrambling back, he knocked over the table and fell. Still screaming, he scooted back on his butt, knocking over more chairs and pushing the tables. He scrambled to his feet and tried to climb over a table, only for it to fall over. His legs got caught up in another chair and he fell again.

Looking back over his shoulder he saw four figures approaching him. All were tall and thin, with arms and legs out of proportion. Their heads were large and gray, with huge brown eyes that angled unnaturally. Each held long tubes, which Chuck assumed were weapons. He gathered this in a glance as he continued yelling. He turned towards his attackers and scooted back on his butt until he was stopped by a wall and the jumble of chairs and tables. The four of them towered over him as he crouched against the wall, screaming. One of them raised his arm up to his face and

Chuck knew this was the end.

Lt. Turner burst into the room, wearing only a pair of boxers and a t-shirt. The four aliens turned towards him and Lt. Turner came to a stop and slowly raised his hands chest high. "Hello, I am Liam," he was saying as Chuck finally stopped yelling. The rest of the trainees started filling the room, but froze when they saw the aliens.

"Everyone, stay where you are," Lt. Turner said to the trainees. He turned back to the aliens. "Can you understand me?" The aliens did not respond. "Is one of you Sally?" The aliens still did not respond, but just stood there. "Damn," Lt. Turner muttered. He touched the bracelet he always wore on his left wrist. "Paul, Paul. Do you copy?" he said. "Paul?"

Fifteen long seconds later, Captain Paul's voice came from the band. "Yes."

"We have a situation here at base. Four Delorians are in the break room and the trainees have stumbled into them. It's a bit of a mess."

"Keep everyone calm," Captain Paul said. "I will be there in five."

"Roger." Lt. Turner turned back to the door. Spotting Carlos, he said, "Carlos, go to my bunk. In a small gray box in the drawer of my nightstand is a small circular patch the size of a dime. Get it and bring it here. Quickly," Lt Turner added.

Carlos squeezed through the trainees blocking

the door and bolted. Lt. Turner walked slowly towards Chuck, who was still crouched on the floor, his back to the wall. Lt. Turner stepped between two of the Delorians, who let him pass without reacting. He knelt down next to Chuck. Chuck's eyes were wide and his breathing was coming in fast gasps.

"It's okay, Chuck," Lt. Turner said quietly. "These are Delorians. They are friends. They aren't going to hurt you," He hoped that was true and wondered why the Delorians were holding large pipe like objects. Captain Paul better get here fast, he thought.

Carlos came back into the room. "I got it," he said, holding out his hand while eyeing the Delorians.

"Bring it here," Lt. Turner said, afraid to leave Chuck, who looked like he would start screaming again. "Slowly."

Carlos walked over slowly, never taking his eyes off the Delorians. He handed Lt. Turner the patch, who placed it behind his left ear and stood and faced the Delorians. Carlos stood there, not knowing what to do. The rest of the trainees were clustered against the wall or in the doorway.

Lt. Turner's mouth moved and he appeared to be talking to the Delorians, but no sound could be heard. A minute later Captain Paul pushed his way through the group and entered the room, wearing his traditional polo shirt, khaki pants and top siders. He walked over to the Delorians and appeared to talk to them, but again no sound could be heard. The Delorians walked back to the cabinet and put down the long tubes and then came back to stand next to Captain Paul.

"Is he hurt?" Captain Paul asked Lt. Turner, referring to Chuck, who was still crouched on the floor.

"I don't think so," Lt. Turner responded. "Just shook up."

Turning to the trainees clustered in the doorway, Captain Paul said, "This is not exactly how I intended to introduce you to the Delorians. However, since we are all here, why don't you all go back into the classroom and take your seats so we can continue this in a more orderly fashion." The trainees backed out of the room, with many surreptitious glances at the Delorians. "Carlos, help Lt. Turner take Chuck into the classroom," Captain Paul said, before turning back to the Delorians.

Carlos and Lt. Turner helped Chuck stand up and walked him into the classroom. Then Captain Paul led the four Delorians to the stage at the front of the classroom. He adjusted something on his wrist and then turned to the trainees.

"Ladies and Gentlemen, may I introduce you to our Delorian friends. I will not insult them by trying to pronounce their names since humans, or at least this human, cannot pronounce most Delorian words. These four can now hear and understand you as I have a translation program operating through this device." He held up his wrist. "However, you cannot hear or understand them unless you have a communication patch, which Lt. Turner and I are both wearing." He pointed to a small patch behind his ear.

"The Delorians were here tonight to install a galley in the break room," Captain Paul continued, pointing to the open door to the other room. "They are putting in food synthesizers, which should be a vast improvement to our MRE's. Evidently Trainee Williams walked in on them, which must have been a bit of a shock. You will not have much contact with the Delorians at this base. But at our next base we will be working side by side with them, so I want to clear up any misunderstandings right now."

Captain Paul fixed his attention on the back of the room. "Trainee Williams."

"Yes, Sir," Williams said a bit weakly.

"The Delorians tell me they were working in the galley when a human came into the room and called out to them. They say they walked out from behind the galley and," Captain Paul paused. "And here I am quoting, 'the human started a high-pitched squealing and started running into the chairs and tables.'" Chuckles ran through the classroom. "Is that an accurate representation of what occurred?"

"I am not sure about the squealing, Sir," Williams responded unhappily.

"That may be a translation glitch," Captain Paul conceded. "But is their report otherwise accurate? Did they attack you?"

The class turned to look at Williams. "They came at me," Williams said. "And they had weapons, or something in their hands."

Captain Paul turned to the Delorians. A moment passed where it appeared he was talking. Then he turned to Williams. "These are technicians," Captain Paul explained. "They say that when they came out, they were holding some conduit and tubing they had been installing." Captain Paul paused again. "Did they ever threaten you with those items?"

"One did raise his hand, Sir."

"Could he have been talking into a communication device like this one?" Captain Paul raised his wrist.

"Possibly, Sir."

"Did they ever try to strike you?"

"No, Sir."

"Good. So, is it safe to say you walked into the break room and when the Delorians walked out you were, shall I say, a bit shocked when four aliens suddenly appeared, rather than one of your classmates. And you then beat a rather hasty, but perhaps ineffective retreat?" Some more chuckles sounded from the room.

"Yes, Sir."

Captain Paul turned and appeared to converse with the Delorians again. Turning back to Williams, he said, "They say they did not intend to scare you and apologize for your fright." When Williams did not respond, Captain Paul added, "Perhaps you would like to accept their apology so they know there are no hard feelings between us."

"Uh, Yes. Of course. Uh," Williams stammered. "Tell them…"

"They can hear and understand you," Captain Paul interrupted.

"Oh, right. Thank you," Williams said. "I understand you meant me no harm and I am sorry that I… overreacted. I was a bit… surprised."

Lt. Turner, who was listening to both sides of the exchange through his patch, could have sworn he saw a smile flit across Captain Paul's face when he talked to the Delorians next. Captain Paul turned back to the class. "Trainee Williams, the Delorians would like to thank you for your understanding. They have asked to greet you formally. Their way of greeting is to exchange a hug. It is very simple. It is also an honor. Would you please come up here and greet the Delorians?"

Although Captain Paul phrased his request as a question, perhaps for the Delorians' translation, it was clearly an order, and Williams understood it as such. Reluctantly, he stood up and slowly walked to the front of the classroom. Lt. Turner thought it looked like the hardest twenty feet Williams had ever walked and hoped that the Delorians did not notice the obvious reluctance. Williams walked to the front and stiffly stood as each of the Delorians approached him and leaned down and gave him a brief hug. When they had finished, Paul sent Williams back to his chair, before turning to the remaining trainees.

"The Delorians asked me to tell you they apologize for their abruptness, but they need to finish the fabricator so they can leave before sunrise." The Delorians turned to leave the stage.

"Attention on deck," Captain Paul announced.

Startled, the trainees jumped to attention and stood there as the Delorians went back to the break room and closed the door. Lt. Turner smiled to himself as he watched the trainees stand at attention, some dressed only in underwear, others with hastily put on shorts or pants. It was a mix-matched group. When the Delorians had left, Captain Paul told the group to sit down.

"Now you have met the Delorians," he started. "And Williams, I commend you for pulling it back together so quickly. You did admirably. And for the rest of you, hopefully when you meet the Delorians the next time, you will be better prepared. And you will have communication patches." Captain Paul looked around the room. "So, does anyone still doubt my story that aliens exist?"

Heads shook as nervous laughter filled the room.

"I don't think Williams will ever doubt it again," someone said, prompting more laughter.

"The good news is that tomorrow morning," Captain Paul said as he looked at his watch, "okay, this morning, you can have breakfast in the break room. Hopefully, you will find it to be superior to MRE's. Now, I think I can get home and get a couple hours of sleep before I come back here. I suspect that after tonight's little episode, most of you won't be able to get back to sleep." He paused and looked around the room.

"Lt. Turner, please make sure that no one goes into the break room the rest of the night. We have had enough excitement for one night." With that, Captain Paul stepped off the stage and headed for the door.

"Attention on deck," Lt. Turner said belatedly, but Captain Paul waved everyone back down before they had a chance to jump to attention.

When Captain Paul left, the trainees milled around the classroom discussing the events. Several walked over to Chuck Williams, who was recounting what happened. "It was like a horror movie," he was saying. "Suddenly four aliens were surrounding me and I couldn't get away. I kept tripping over those damn chairs…"

Katie and Donna were standing off to the side listening. "I think 'Squealer' should be his new call sign," Donna whispered to Katie.

"Definitely," Katie agreed.

* * *

"No more MRE's," Lt. Turner told the group the next morning after PT. "From now on we are eating in the break room. Despite last night's little interruption, the Delorians finished installing the food converters."

"Oh, great, alien food," John said.

Lt. Turner led them through the classroom into the break room and to the back wall where the food converter had been installed. "You put your hand on the screen here," Lt. Turner instructed while pointing to the screen. "This will pull up a menu of items. You can select your item by pressing on it, or you can just order it verbally. Your A.I.'s have access to this computer.

"Al," Lt. Turner said, speaking to the screen. "I'll have an omelet with cheese, mushrooms and onions, please. And orange juice on the side." There was a short conveyer belt coming out the side. A tray came out with a hot omelet and a glass of orange juice.

Lt. Turner picked it up, walked to a side unit where utensils were stored and headed for a nearby table. "Try your luck," he said as he sat down. Several trainees queued around the dispenser, while a few skeptics followed Lt. Turner to his table.

"What?" he asked as he looked up at the group around him.

"I just want to see if it is edible first," Sarah said.

"Yea, eat up, Sir. We'll see if you die first," Katie said with a laugh.

Lt. Turner dug his fork into the omelet and tasted it. He grabbed his throat and gagged. When he saw the look of shock on their faces, he started laughing.

"Nice theatrics," Sarah said.

"It actually isn't bad," Lt. Turner admitted.

The rest of the trainees were ordering their food.

"Oh, man," John Ericson said as he dug into his omelet. "This sure beats MRE's."

"It's really not that bad," Donna said.

"Not bad?" John replied. "It's great."

"Well, we now know who can't cook," Donna said, earning a laugh from several trainees within earshot. "It's not home cooking, but it is not bad. Certainly better than MRE's," she conceded.

"We will definitely have to keep up our PT

schedule now that we are eating real food," Chuck said.

The break room filled with the smell of eggs, bacon and coffee. The banter continued until they finished and headed back to the classroom for the next round of VR training.

# CHAPTER FIFTEEN

"This is the stealth module..."

"This is the navigation module..."

"This is the propulsion module..."

Each module started the same as the trainees were inundated with more information than they thought they could possibly retain. Each day was the same: morning PT, followed by breakfast, then VR training followed by more PT, then repeat.

They were told they had Sunday off, but since they couldn't go anywhere, many opted to continue VR training, wondering when they would be shown flight controls.

At 1530 hours on Sunday, Lt. Turner called the group together for an impromptu meeting.

"Can any of you ride horses?" Captain Paul asked the assembled group of trainees without any preamble. "And I don't mean sit on a western saddle and go wherever the horse decides to go," Captain Paul continued. "I mean really ride. Anyone here ride English or is a real cowboy?"

Four hands went up, three women and one man. Katie Jerguson rode cattle on her grandfather's ranch back in Texas, Donna Peterson showed hunter/jumper as a kid, Teddy Watson had done low level dressage during high school and college, and Catherine Miller had grown up on a horse farm, riding English and jumping.

"These are your new section leaders," Captain Paul continued, pointing to Katie, Donna and Teddy, who were sitting near the front of the room. Catherine was sitting near the back wall. We will have three groups of ten. Fall out into the hangar bay. Section leaders, pick your sections and then report back here. You have five minutes."

In four and a half minutes the section leaders reported back to Captain Paul in the classroom. The three sat in chairs at the front of the classroom, while the Captain and Lt. Turner stood at the front of the room.

"We are going on a road trip," Captain Paul said. "The whole group is enrolled in a six-day, intensive dressage class at the University of Virginia's Equestrian Center. We will be staying at the Army's Judge Advocate General's School, which is on the University's campus right next to the law school. We will spend our days at The Barracks, which is not an army facility, but rather a private farm where the equestrian team trains."

Captain Paul looked at the confused faces. "We have to expand our abilities. In an aircraft you have a stick, a throttle — the collective for you rotary wing types — and two peddles. You master those and the rest follows. That won't work to fly the Delorian fighters. They were not designed for humans. Simply pushing pedals with your feet will not be sufficient to fly them."

"But we only have two arms and legs," Teddy objected. "And so do the Delorians."

"Yes, but they use them differently. Which is why you will be taking dressage lessons," Captain Paul said. "Most people think all there is to riding a horse is to sit on the saddle, kick them, yell 'yah' and steer with the reins. As you know, there is so much more. You guide the horse with your legs, give commands with your calves, thighs, even your butt muscles. Just how you sit communicates with the horse. The reins are the least of your communication aides. I bet you all could guide your horses without touching the reins."

The three equestrians nodded.

"I was the human test pilot for these fighters. And fortunately or unfortunately for our trainees, I also rode English, having schooled in dressage and jumping. The Delorians modified the controls of these fighters to respond to commands much like a horse. So human pilots must be able to isolate their muscles, to independently give commands with one leg or another or by butt muscles, just like riding a horse. That is not an easy skill to learn. Think back to when you first learned to ride a horse. The best way I know of teaching that is to give our trainees dressage lessons, where the horses will give them instant feedback to let them know if they are doing it right or not."

What Captain Paul did not say was that Liam was the guinea pig for how the training was being conducted as he usually received the training a day or two before anyone else. The A.I.'s would then modify the regimen according to how Liam responded. Things had been progressing well until Liam had to fly the fighter using his whole body. The concept was just too foreign. Paul had demonstrated it numerous times, making the fighter dance across the sky by merely shifting his weight, but Liam could not reproduce it. It was like trying to rub his stomach and pat his head, he had complained. And that is how the dressage lessons came to be. And like everything else in this program, Paul had to rush to make it work.

Paul had contacted UVA's riding team coach and by offering a rather sizable 'donation,' arranged for a last minute, one-week intensive course for his pilots. The cover story was that the General for the Air Cavalry, who Paul reluctantly admitted was a bit eccentric, wanted all his pilots to understand what true cavalry was like, and since dressage started as cavalry training, here they were. Paul obtained housing for a week at the Army JAGC school at UVA as the JAG school was between courses and had rooms available.

Orders authorizing their use were easily provided by the Delorians hacking the military computers. Another set of orders diverted an Air Force plane to transport his pilots to Charlottesville. After that, he chartered a private bus to transport his people from the airport to the University and then to and from The Barracks. Fortunately, money was not a problem with the Delorians. Paul had finished the details about noon on Sunday.

"You will have some very sore puppies in a couple of days," Donna was saying, interrupting Paul's thoughts as he tried to determine whether he had forgotten anything. "They will be using muscles they never used before."

"Yea, like holding on to the horse with their legs for dear life," Katie laughed. "They are going to be crippled by Wednesday."

"That is probably true," Captain Paul said distractedly as he scrolled through his iPad. "Section leaders, get with Lt. Turner. We will have a shipment of paddock boots, half chaps, riding pants, gloves and helmets, waiting for us in Charlottesville. In the meantime, get everyone ready to go. Civilian clothes and Class B uniforms. Outfit everyone for one week. We leave tomorrow at 0500. We will have a formation tonight at 1700 hours. Until then, dismissed."

At 1700 hours the pilots were assembled in the classroom. Captain Paul strode to the front of the classroom. "Here's the deal. From initial tests, it is apparent that only four people here have a prayer of learning to fly the Delorian fighters. They are your three section leaders and Catherine Miller. That is unacceptable and we are going to remedy it. The problem is that the fighters cannot be flown like human aircraft with a hand on the stick and two leg peddles. They require input from your whole body. You will have to learn to control your muscles so they work independently and can provide separate and identifiable cues."

"The fastest way I know to teach you to do that is to have you learn to ride a horse. And I don't mean some dead head trail horse. You are going to learn dressage. For those of you who don't know what that is, I have a video clip for you." A video started on the screen behind Paul. "This is Goncalo Carvalho performing in the 2012 Olympics in London." Captain Paul paused while the students watched the video. "Watch the rider," he instructed. "Tell me how he is getting the horse to move." Captain Paul let them watch the full six and one-half minute performance.

The horse and rider entered a groomed dirt arena twenty by sixty meters. Music was playing in the background. The rider saluted the judges and then the performance began. At first the horse just trotted forward and only an equestrian would recognize that the horse's steps were choreographed. But soon it pranced sideways, crossing its legs as it did so. The horse trotted, pranced in place, did a 360-degree circle without its back legs moving from one spot, and hi-stepped around the ring.

"How did he get the horse to do that?" one of the trainees muttered in disbelief.

"He didn't move," another said.

"His hands were moving," someone else said.

"No, his hands were moving with the horse," another corrected.

"Play it again," Captain Paul instructed when the video ended. "We are very used to doing everything with our hands," Captain Paul explained as the video played a second time. "That is too limiting. Here Carvalho is doing subtle moves with his hands, primarily his fingers, but most of his commands are done with his seat or legs." Captain Paul paused as the tape continued. "Watch this half pass. The horse is responding to his leg and his seat. You have to give commands independently from every part of your body. If the commands are confusing, then the horse does not know what to do. Well trained horses, like this beauty, want to do what you ask them. But you have to be clear in your instructions. You have to support them. You are not going to force a 1,200-pound horse to do anything. You have to ask, and as demonstrated here, it can be very subtle, yet with very dramatic results." Captain Paul let the tape play to the end again.

"I don't expect any of you to compete in the Olympics after this week. In fact, most of you will be too sore to walk in a couple days. But what I do expect, is that you will learn to isolate your muscles. You will learn to give independent commands with your heels, calves, thighs and butt muscles. How you shift your weight in the saddle is a command. And the horses will let you know immediately if you have learned this technique. They will either do what you ask or buck your butt off." A nervous laugh filled the room. "There is no cheating on a horse. No faking it. You have to communicate with your horse while trying to stay on his back at a trot and not fall off. You can't hold on with your hands and you can't squeeze with your legs, because that is a command also. A command to run, by the way."

"Your X.O. has often informed me that my training requirements are confusing. And I will admit that is often true. After all, we are dealing with aliens and alien technology and we have to adapt as we go along. I will try to explain this simply. Every movement that horse made, going straight, sideways, spinning in a circle, backing up, the Delorian fighter can do. And it can do it at incredible speed, in three dimensions and upside down. If you have to think about flying, you are dead. You will have to fly by reflex and with your whole body. The cockpit has been designed to read and respond to your every movement from your head down to your toes. So, it is vitally important that you are aware of your movements and can independently control them."

"You better not sneeze while flying this fighter," one of the trainees whispered.

Captain Paul ignored the comment. "You have to master this. If you can't, then you can't fly the Delorian fighter. It is that simple."

Captain Paul paused as he watched the assembled pilots, trying to gauge their reaction. Some seemed skeptical. Others seemed confused. "You will be cursing me in a day or two when you have saddle sores and can barely walk," Captian Paul continued. "You think I joke? I took a week-long polo clinic at this very same facility. On Wednesday I could barely walk. But on Friday I was hitting the winning goal. It is doable. You just won't believe it, not for the first couple of days, anyway."

# CHAPTER SIXTEEN

"Why does the military do everything at 0-dark-thirty?" Carlos complained, as he and his colleagues lay on the hangar floor, resting on their duffel bags. It was 0430 and even the birds had not started chirping. At 0440 Captain Paul walked into the hangar. Most did not notice him until Lt. Turner shouted, "Attention on Deck."

"As you were," Captain Paul said, as the trainees were struggling to their feet. "Listen up," he continued. "There is a C-130 five minutes out. I actually passed it coming in."

"I hope he had stealth mode on," Carlos whispered. "Can you imagine the pilot's reaction if he saw a gold Honda passing him at 10,000 feet?" A couple of trainees in earshot chuckled.

"Lt. Turner will issue you these communication bands." He held up a black band that looked like a silicon remembrance band. These are similar to what Lt. Turner and I wear. Never take them off. And I mean never. If anyone asks, they are a remembrance band for fellow service members lost in battle. Which is fitting, since they will monitor your vitals. Think of them as a fitbit on steroids. I'll tell you more about them later."

"Remember, this is a black operation. No one knows about us. You have to keep it that way. Your section leaders have told you the cover story. Stick to it and keep it vague. You can talk about all of your military training up to the point you joined this squadron. Do not talk about anything that you have seen, heard, or done in the last week at all. Not even privately with each other. The NSA has a lot of monitoring devices and aliens is one of their key words. What we don't know is who or what may be monitoring the NSA. Red Force may have a spy satellite out there that we are not aware of. We are blocked here by Delorian tech. You will not be once you step foot on that C-130. Do not use phones or computers while we are out. If you want to talk to anyone other than the people we have to interact with for food, travel, lodging or training, check with Lt. Turner or me first." Captain Paul paused as he looked out over the trainees.

"Operational security, folks. It does not get any more serious than this. We cannot let Red Force have any idea what we are doing. Our whole plan is based upon the element of surprise. Let's keep it that way."

As Captain Paul finished his speech, a plane

could be heard in the distance.

"Looks like your ride finally got here," Captain Paul said. "I'll see you in Virginia." With that he walked out of the hangar. The trainees picked up their gear and headed out the door after him. Those first out the door saw Captain Paul climb into his gold Honda, which promptly disappeared.

"I have got to get me one of those Honda's," Sarah joked.

"Yea, certainly beats a Corvette any day," Jeffrey said.

"Sure does," Sarah agreed.

The C-130 came lumbering in and stopped at the end of the runway. The trainees marched to the plane and climbed up the back ramp. Minutes later they were wheels up. Not having anything else to do, most of the trainees went back to sleep.

They arrived in Charlottesville at 0730 and were finding their rooms at the JAG school by 0800. They had thirty minutes to unpack, eat, find and put on the riding clothes that had been delivered for them and be ready for the bus to take them to The Barracks for the start of their dressage class. Most of them climbed on the bus without having had time for breakfast.

At 0850 the charter bus pulled onto the grounds of The Barracks and dropped off the trainees. As the trainees stepped off the bus they were greeted with the smell of crisp air and the scenic view of green fields surrounded by Virginia mountains.

"I love this crisp air," Alex said as the group walked toward the barn.

"You don't miss the 1,000% humidity we have on the Gulf Coast?" Katie joked back.

"This is the life," Patrick said.

Donna laughed. "They will be changing their tune by Wednesday when they can't walk," she said to Teddy, who nodded his head in agreement.

"Hey, look," Phillip said, pointing to a familiar gold Honda parked near the barn. "I wonder how he got here?" Several trainees laughed at the inside joke.

They were met at the barn by Captain Paul, who was dressed in his customary polo shirt and khaki's. He introduced them to their new instructor. "This is Julie Dawson. She will be your chief riding instructor. Consider her your new drill sergeant."

"That won't be far off," Donna whispered to Teddy as they stood in the back of the group.

"I don't know why they are making such a big deal of this?" Phillip whispered to Karen. "How hard can it be to sit on a horse. I mean, really. It's not like you are doing anything. We do PT two and three times a day."

"Section leaders, front and center," Captain

Paul said and Teddy, Katie and Donna moved to the front of the group. "Catherine Miller, you too." Captain Paul introduced the section leaders and Catherine to Julie, offering their assistance if needed. They broke into sections, designated Alpha Section, Bravo and Charlie, with Liam assigned to Alpha. Each section was assigned a lead instructor and also a couple of UVA equestrian team members to help coach. All told, there were ten instructors assigned to the trainees, with the possibility of more as the week progressed.

"He may have set this up at the last minute," Teddy remarked to Donna as they stood to the side of the group, "but he sure did get it organized well. Look at all this support staff." Donna nodded in agreement.

Julie was at the front of the group now. She was giving the orientation speech, pointing out the location of the barn, stalls, paddocks, break room, indoor and outdoor arena's and the all important bathrooms. "We will rotate your three sections through the classroom sections and the riding sections. Your horses will be groomed and tacked for you, so you will not have to do that. You just have to learn to ride."

"I can see the classroom now," Daniel whispered. "This is a horse. This is the front end, this is the back. You sit here."

Julie led the group into an large indoor arena where they were instructed to have a seat on metal bleachers overlooking a dirt arena. A young college girl, wearing knee high black boots, riding pants, shirt and a riding helmet was trotting a horse around the ring. The horse's head was bowed down as it moved smartly around in a twenty-meter circle, while the rider sat motionless on the saddle.

Captain Paul was standing next to Julie and spoke next. "Since you are all goal driven individuals and since I suspect most of you still don't truly understand why you are here, we are going to show you the test you have to pass by the end of the week. That way you can properly focus on what to learn." He turned and nodded to Julie.

Julie called out to the rider that she could begin.

The horse and rider moved to the center of the arena, facing the trainees. She stopped and stood still and then nodded her head to the crowd. She then walked her horse forward toward the group. When she approached the wall, the horse turned to the right and broke into a slow trot. She trotted around the arena, the horse's head bowed and bent in slightly, while she posted the trot. When she completed the lap, she trotted diagonally across the arena.

"There's the diagonal change," Teddy whispered as the horse and rider passed the center of the arena.

"What's that?" Teresa asked.

"You change how you post depending on what direction you are going," Teddy said.

"I still don't know what you mean."

"Shhh," Daniel said.

The rider had completed a circuit going the other direction and was now trotting a twenty-meter circle.

"She's sitting the trot now," Teddy said. "She's not posting. Not going up and down," he added exasperatedly when Teresa kept looking at him with a blank look.

By now the horse and rider had completed two circles and the horse broke into a canter and cantered around the ring, first in one direction and then in the other. When they had finished, they proceeded to the center of the ring, where they stopped and the rider nodded to the crowd.

Captain Paul stood up and faced the trainees. "I hope you noticed that was not the same as the dressage performance I showed you last night. What you just saw was a beautiful demonstration of basic English riding, in the walk, trot and canter. You have to know that to ride English."

"I still don't see the big deal," Daniel whispered. "How hard can it be?"

"That was part one," Captain Paul said, almost as if answering Daniel. "But you have to master part two if you are going to complete this course. Watch carefully." He nodded to Julie as he sat down. Julie nodded to the rider and sat down also.

The trainees watched as another UVA student walked up and slid the horses bridle off its head and walked back to the side of the arena. Without any reins, the rider sat up and put her hands behind her back, while the horse just stood there quietly. She nodded to the crowd and then the horse walked forward. When it got to the wall, it turned and started to trot, while the rider remained sitting straight, her hands behind her back. The trainees watched as the rider repeated the whole course with her hands behind her back the whole time, ending once again with a complete stop in the middle of the arena.

When the rider nodded to the crowd, Teddy clapped enthusiastically, and then stopped when no one else clapped. Captain Paul stood up and clapped and then turned to the trainees. "That was a very impressive performance," he said, both to the trainees and Julie. Turning back to the trainees, he added, "You have no idea how difficult that is, but you are about to find out. You have some excellent instructors here and some damn fine horses. This is not a vacation folks. I expect each of you to master this training by the end of the week. That is a huge ask, but I believe you can do it." He then turned to Julie. "Ms. Dawson, they are all yours."

# CHAPTER SEVENTEEN

Liam did not know what to expect. Having come from the city, he had never ridden a horse before. It looked easy in the movies, but that was the movies. Paul had assured him he could do it, but by Wednesday, he would be real sore. Liam was with Alpha section and he and the ten members of Alpha, led by Teddy Watson, were assigned to one of the waiting UVA students. She led them outside and over to a grassy area near a fence, where two other female UVA students were waiting, one sitting on a horse a couple of yards away.

"My name is Jenna," the first student introduced herself. "This is Ray and riding Blaze is Joanna. Have any of you ridden a horse before?"

Teddy raised his hand. "I competed dressage in high school and college up to First Level," he said.

The three girls were obviously impressed. "Good," Jenna said. "You can help us instruct." She turned to the rest of the group. "I'll start with the basics. Safety. These are good horses, but they are horses. Do no frighten them."

"Frighten them?" Jeffrey whispered to Patrick. "They frighten me, look how big they are.

"Do not make quick movements or loud noises around them," Jenna continued. "Don't just reach up to pat them on the head, the sudden movement could scare them. They weigh twelve hundred pounds, you don't. They have metal shoes on. You don't. Keep your feet out of their way. And never, ever, step behind a horse. Their natural defense is to kick. If you frighten them, they will kick."

"This is going to be fun," Alex whispered.

Jenna held up what looked like coils of leather straps with a silver metal attachment. "This is a bridle. As you saw in the demonstration, a good rider does not need reins to control a horse. In fact the reins are only a small part of what controls a horse. But more of that later. The bridle holds the bit," she held up the metal part of the bridle, "which fits in their mouths. The bit is controlled by the reins. You have to be very gentle with the reins. The bit gives aids. Gentle aids. If you yank on the reins, if you pull hard on the reins, it hurts the horse's mouth. They will object. They will not do what you want them to do. If they get upset enough, they will buck you off. These are very well-trained horses. They are sweet horses. If they buck you off, you deserve it. You will also be ruining their training. So the key is to be soft with your hands."

"So far all they said is be careful about the horse, nothing about us," Chuck complained quietly.

"That's because they care more about the horse than you," Sarah replied.

"The first thing we will do is to show you how to get on a horse and walk and trot," Jenna said.

Joanna climbed off the horse and then walked it over to a mounting block that was basically two steps made out of molded plastic. She had the horse stand next to the block. "Observe," Jenna was saying. "Forget anything you have ever seen about riding horses in western movies. We don't jump onto horses, we don't yank on the saddle and we don't yell 'yah.' You climb up on the mounting block, place a foot in the stirrup and lift yourself into the saddle with your leg, not your arms. And then you sit, gently, on the saddle. You don't flop down on their backs."

Joanna demonstrated as Jenna narrated. They then described how to sit on the horse. "Keep your back straight, heels down. Don't crouch over the horse." Joanna continued to demonstrate, showing how to walk and then how to post a trot. When they had finished, Jenna turned to the group. "We have three horses, so we can work three people at a time. We can do one in the round pen and two on lunge lines. Who wants to go first?"

As section leader, Teddy turned to his group. "I think Lt. Turner should get to lead the way, don't you?" Teddy addressed the group. Laughing, they all agreed.

Lt. Turner reluctantly walked up to Jenna. "You can call me Liam," he said to Jenna.

Sarah and Pat volunteered as well.

Joanna led the horse and Lt. Turner into the round pen, which was basically a deep sandy ring about twenty meters in diameter, surrounded by five-foot high wooden rails. There was a mounting block in the center and Joanna led the horse next to it. Several trainees watched Lt. Turner climb on the horse, while others watched Sarah and Pat.

"Sit up straight, heels down," Joanna instructed as she tied the reins in a knot and lay them on the horse's neck.

"What do I do with the reins?" Liam asked.

"Nothing. You don't get reins yet."

"Then how do I control the horse?"

"With your body," she answered as she led the horse to the side of the round pen. She walked back to the center of the round pen and picked up a lunge whip.

Liam looked at the whip with concern.

"Put your hands down by your sides and gently squeeze the horse with your calves," Joanna instructed.

Liam thought he complied, but the horse did not move. He squeezed some more. Nothing.

Then he was rocked back when the horse started walking, almost losing his balance and somehow resisted grabbing the horse's mane. He thought he had made the horse move until he saw that Joanna had moved the lunge whip behind the horse, prompting him to walk. Paul was right, this was as bad as trying to fly the fighter, Liam thought.

Joanna told him to stop by sitting down and leaning just slightly back. 'I am sitting down,' Liam thought. 'And if I lean back anymore, I will fall off the horse.' He tried and the horse kept walking around in the circle until Joanna moved the lunge whip in front of the horse and it stopped.

Joanna went through the instructions again, this time telling Liam to lean slightly forward when he squeezed and make a 'clicking' sound with his mouth.

"No, 'yah'," Liam tried to joke. Joanna just shook her head and Liam leaned forward and squeezed his lower legs. Nothing happened so he tried again, this time squeezing as hard as he could as he clicked. The horse leaped forward and Liam rolled right off his back, landing in a heap in the soft sand while the onlookers laughed and hooted. Liam scrambled to his feet before the horse came around and ran over him. Brushing sand off, he saw the horse was quietly standing on the other side of the ring.

"Why did you kick him?" Joanna was saying. "There is no need to be rough. I said squeeze."

"I'm fine, thank you," Liam said as he finished brushing himself off. He felt his face turning red as the others laughed. Then he had to get back on and try again. He managed to stay on the rest of his lesson and finally got the horse to walk without Joanna using the lunge whip. However, he never could get him to stop by command.

Fortunately for Liam's ego, the rest of the section fared about the same, except for Teddy who looked like he was born on a horse, riding smooth and relaxed. He got the horse to walk, trot, canter and stop, all without reins and without seeming to move at all. After Teddy had climbed off Blaze and patted him affectionately, Liam walked up and asked him how he had done it.

"Years of training," Teddy answered.

"We don't have years," Liam objected. "We have a week."

"The key is to relax," Teddy said. "When you were riding you were really stiff and each step just bounced you in the saddle. You have to relax, sink into the saddle, into the horse until you and the horse move as one."

Liam shook his head. He could not imagine how he could relax while trying not to fall off and giving commands at the same time. This was going to be a long week.

A catering truck arrived at lunch time and everyone milled around, choosing the various sandwiches and salads that it offered.

"This sure beats MRE's," Carlos said as he dug into a roast beef sandwich on an onion bun. "Hey, Lt. Turner, do you think you can talk Captain Paul into having this truck cater the base?"

"Wouldn't that be great," Brenda agreed.

Captain Paul had stayed to watch the training and now invited the staff to join them for lunch. Soon, fifteen UVA students were lining up for food.

"Are all equestrian clubs all female," Chuck asked Teddy as he looked around at all the UVA students.

"Not all," Teddy said. "But the vast majority of them are."

"And you did this for years?"

"High school and college."

"Oh, man. You had it made."

"I was the only guy, surrounded by lots of girls," Teddy admitted. "Of course, most of them cared more about their horses than me."

"Most?"

"Yes, most. But not all." Teddy smiled.

"I should have joined an equestrian club."

The afternoon was more of the same, with the groups rotating between classroom, horses and break time. Liam rode two more times and managed to stay on both times and get his horse to walk and trot. Staying on at the trot was a challenge even while posting. "Let the horse bring you up out of the saddle," his instructor said. Liam just felt like he was bouncing up and down on the horse.

The charter bus arrived at 1700 to take them back to the JAG school. As the trainees climbed into the bus, Captain Paul motioned Lt. Turner over. "Ride with me," he said.

Lt. Turner climbed into the passenger seat of the gold Honda.

"Al, follow the bus," Paul said when Liam closed the door. The Honda dutifully followed the bus.

Liam wondered if he would ever get used to the Delorian tech.

"What do you think?" Paul asked. "About the dressage training," Paul added, when Liam did not respond.

"I don't know," Liam said. "You were certainly correct about the horses letting you know when you get it wrong."

"I heard you fell off," Paul said. "Don't feel bad, I've come off a lot. It's part of the experience. How about using your legs? Did that make any sense?"

"Honestly, not yet," Liam said. "Intellectually, I think I understand what they are saying, but right now I just don't get it. I don't see how I am going to pass that test at the end of the week with reins, let alone without them."

"How about the others?"

"Teddy has it down, that's for sure," Liam answered. "He was so relaxed, he looked like he was part of the horse. He should make a greater fighter pilot," Liam answered with just a note of envy.

"Don't worry," Paul said. "You will get it. Just keep trying and suddenly it will click and everything will make sense."

"I hope so."

"It will," Paul assured him. "Now when we get to the JAG school, have them change and take them for a run."

"PT? After today? Are you kidding?" Liam asked.

"Trust me. It is going to get a lot worse and jogging will help loosen the muscles. Don't go very fast and only a couple miles. Just to stay loose. We will do the same thing every night, although I predict that Wednesday night will be a crawl, not a run. Then have them clean up, dinner is at the O-Club, top floor, at 1900. After that, they can relax. Breakfast starts tomorrow at the O-Club at 0700, bus leaves at 0800. If they want to train VR, I have the units in the trunk here. They can check them out with you, but they have to check them back with you when they finish. It won't work for anyone else, but I still don't want this tech lying around."

"Anything else?" Liam asked as the car pulled up to the JAG school.

"Yes, tell Teddy that I will come by his room at 2200. I'm going to see if you are right, that he can fly a fighter. Don't tell him that last part. Just tell him I need to see him."

Liam suppressed a pang of jealousy.

"I'll need you to fly the shuttle," Paul added. "We will fly out tandem. Now go have fun at PT."

"You're not joining us for PT?" Liam asked jokingly.

"I'm sure I can find a hot tub around here that will feel much better," Paul replied. "However, I have to make sure I keep the logistics for all this fun running smoothly. I'll meet you at your room at 2145 hours.

# CHAPTER EIGHTEEN

Promptly at 2200 hours there was a knock on Teddy's door. He was expecting it, but did not know what Captain Paul wanted. When he opened his door, both Captain Paul and Lt. Turner were standing in the hallway. Lt. Turner had a package under his arm.

"Good evening," Captain Paul said. "May we come in?"

"Oh, yes, certainly, Sir," Teddy said as he stepped aside.

Captain Paul and Lt. Turner walked in and Teddy closed the door and turned, still wondering what this was all about.

"Lt. Turner said you rode admirably today," Captain Paul said.

"Yes, Sir. You don't easily forget years of dressage training."

"How would you like to try your skills on a fighter?"

"A fighter? The fighter?" Teddy looked around the room, unsure what to say.

"We are shielded," Captain Paul said, holding up his wrist which had a black arm band, similar to the one the trainees had received, but two inches wide. "I want to give you a test ride. I need to make sure this dressage training we are doing will work. Are you game?"

"Yes, Sir!" Teddy said without hesitation.

"I thought you would be," Captain Paul said. "Put on this spacesuit," he added as Lt. Turner tossed the package he had been holding onto Teddy's bed.

Teddy quickly stripped off his clothes and pulled on the spacesuit. When he had sealed the front, Captain Paul said, "Put your clothes on over the suit and choose a long sleeve shirt. We have to walk past the duty officer in the lobby and it would be hard to explain why you are wearing a dive skin, as Lt. Turner refers to these suits."

As Teddy complied, he realized that both Captain Paul and Lt. Turner had spacesuits on under their clothes, only the top of the black fabric showing at their collar. When he had finished, he looked at his hands, which looked like he was wearing black nylon gloves. "I'll show you later how to detach the gloves," Captain Paul said. "For now, you can be very unmilitary and walk with your hands in your pockets." With that, they escorted Teddy out of his room, down to the lobby and past the duty officer.

Captain Paul's gold Honda was parked outside and they climbed in and Captain Paul drove to a nearby outdoor field where they had done their PT earlier. The field's lights were off and it appeared secluded. "Al, do a perimeter sweep," Captain Paul said.

"Perimeter secure," Al said from the ceiling speaker. No humanoids in line of sight, no active surveillance devices. There is an Oryctolagus Cuniculus observing you from the tree line fifty-two meters away at seventy-eight degrees."

Teddy froze. Was that another alien? Had they been spotted? What were they going to do?

"Let me know if the rabbit makes any hostile moves," Captain Paul said. "Al has a sense of humor," he explained to Teddy. "You have to get used to it." They climbed out of the Honda. "Take off your civilian clothing and give it to Lt. Turner. He will store it in the shuttle for when we come back."

When the clothing had been secured and they were all standing around in their black spacesuits, Teddy looked around for the fighter. Although it was a dark night, his eyes had adjusted and he could see pretty well. They were alone on the field.

"It's over here," Captain Paul said as he walked a few feet away from the shuttle. "Al drop shielding over the access area.

The air in front of them shimmered and Teddy could just make what looked like a gray slide with handholds. He recognized it immediately from the VR training. With Captain Paul in the lead, they climbed up the side of the fighter and dropped down through the top hatch. The fighter was configured for two pilots, and Captain Paul slid down into the left seat and Teddy slid down in the co-pilot seat. The hatch immediately sealed above them.

"Lighting up," Captain Paul said and the cockpit lights came on. All of the control panels remained blank. "You have trained in VR on the control panels, but I need to show you how the seat works. As you can see, it is modeled after an English saddle. Actually, my Devoucoux saddle."

"You had a Devoucoux?" Teddy interrupted. "I always wanted one, but they were too pricey for my budget."

"I found mine at a dealer at the Red Hills Horse Trials in Tallahassee one year. It's a great saddle. I had a Stueben before, which I thought was good, but the Devoucoux beat it hands down. Which is good since you will be spending a lot of time in these fighters and you will want a comfortable seat. You sit in it just like you would a regular saddle. There are stirrups for pedals that you need to adjust to make them comfortable. I would adjust them long, like for dressage, not jump position. You adjust them like this," Captain Paul said while he demonstrated where the adjustment was behind the thigh.

"Once you get that set, you run these straps over your upper thighs. They act like Velcro and hold you in the saddle."

"I could have used those when I was learning to ride," Teddy said, as he adjusted the straps. "Why strap down to the saddle, though?"

"Because in space there is no gravity and if you are going to be giving commands with your legs and butt, you better not float off your seat," Captain Paul explained.

"Good point," Teddy agreed.

"Once you get comfortable in the saddle, then we have to adjust the back of the seat," Captain Paul continued. "You don't have to sit up in the saddle all the time in the fighter. That would be exhausting and would limit the amount of time we could realistically field the fighters. So the fighters have a two part seat, the saddle and the back. The back of the seat does two things: it takes commands from you and it will protect you from sudden movements."

"Lean back into the seat like this," Captain Paul demonstrated. "The seat will mold against you, like a memory foam bed. Now slip your arms through these mesh restraints and seal them across your chest. They act like a shoulder harness. Here comes the interesting part. You can move forward and back and the seatback follows you, like your car seat does when you pull the adjustment lever up. However, you can adjust the resistance of the seat so you barely feel its support, or it locks in place and anywhere in between." Paul demonstrated by leaning forward and then leaning back until he was almost lying flat. "The adjustment for the seat is here by your side, or you can instruct your A.I. to do it for you."

"The seat back will also allow you to move side to side, but not with as much range as front and back." Captain Paul demonstrated again. "When you are flying the fighter, you will sit and move just like you would on a horse, but without the posting. Adjust the seat back so that it gives you as much resistance or feedback as you are comfortable with. You will fly the fighter as if it is part of you, just like you ride a horse. Got it?"

"I guess," Teddy said. "I will really have to try it to tell for sure."

"That's what we are here for," Captain Paul said. "And just FYI, if your fighter takes a hit, the seat will freeze up, just like a seatbelt does on impact, and hopefully protect you from the sudden forces. The A.I. will also cut off seat controls momentarily so getting thrown around in your seat does not send commands to the fighter."

Captain Paul waited while Teddy adjusted and readjusted his seat until he was comfortable with the setting. When he appeared satisfied with the setting, Captain Paul continued. "I'm going to take her out. You can have the seat locked, or you can have it in flight mode. Choice is yours. The inertial dampeners will be on so you will not need the seat for support and the controls on your seat will be deactivated while I pilot."

"Al, activate systems," Captain Paul commanded. The control panels lit up throughout the cockpit and the overhead cockpit light dimmed. "Al, activate external view." The top half of the cockpit suddenly showed the outside view, as if looking out a window. "Enhance, natural lighting." Now the view was as if viewing their surroundings in daytime. Teddy was not surprised as he had done all of this during some of his VR training. "Al, identify your rabbit."

The rabbit appeared, highlighted by an IR sensor. Next to it floated a window with information about its distance from them as well as its size and estimated density. "Target rabbit." A yellow ring appeared over the rabbit with crosshairs over its head. Another window popped up with armament choices and power and distance readings.

"You're not going to shoot the rabbit?" Teddy asked, stunned.

"No," Captain Paul laughed. "Just letting you see the interplay on the displays. "Cancel targeting," Captain Paul continued. "Lay in course." A heads-up display ghosted on the forward "window" showing their projected course in three dimensions. "Lunar One to Lunar Two, ready for lift off?"

"Roger, Lunar One."

"Lunar Two, you are cleared to proceed. We will follow."

"Roger, Lunar One. Lunar Two is clear and taking off now," Lt. Turner responded as the shuttle rose.

Teddy watched the shuttle as it rose from the ground and then pulled up and cleared the trees, rapidly disappearing in the distance. An icon on the forward display screen remained with a pop-up window providing details of the shuttle's flight, including acceleration, speed, altitude and distance from them.

The shuttle was ten miles away and accelerating when Captain Paul launched the fighter, slowly bringing it up over the treetops. Then, without warning and without any sense of movement, they were hurtling through the air. After his initial shock, Teddy looked for the navigation console and saw that they were following the shuttle's path at just under Mach 1. No sense advertising their presence with a sonic boom, Teddy thought.

The fighter banked so that now they were heading straight up into the sky. Teddy twisted in his seat and looked back. The rear display acted like a window, showing the lights on the ground getting smaller. He looked sideways and saw the curvature of the Earth, with the terminator line from the sun in the distance. Then they were in space and the stars shone cold and bright in an absolutely black background. Although he never felt any movement, he realized he was weightless and the practical aspect of being strapped to his seat.

"You can adjust the inertial dampeners to provide you some feedback for your maneuvers," Captain Paul broke the silence. "That way you don't have to rely on just your vision or the console to tell you what the ship is doing. For instance." He adjusted a control and then banked the fighter left, right, up and down. As he did so, Teddy felt his body rocking slightly with the motion. Captain Paul adjusted it again and this time when he turned the ship, the effect was a lot more pronounced inside the cockpit. "Time in the saddle, so to speak, will tell you how much feedback you want."

"Lunar Two, set course Waypoint One, Program One," Captain Paul commanded.

"Roger, Lunar One. Course set, Waypoint One, Program One," Lt. Turner responded.

Captain Paul brought the fighter to a dead stop, while the shuttle continued to travel, visible now only on the sensor display as it was too far to see with the naked eye. Captain Paul turned to Teddy. "Okay, it's your turn. Your first mission is simply to catch up with the shuttle. Al will keep you from hitting it."

"How," Teddy asked. "We haven't gone through flight controls yet."

"Yes, you have," Captain Paul said. "The fighter is your horse. Ride the fighter to the shuttle as you would ride a horse. You just don't have to worry about bringing your horse round or bending its neck, so your hands are free to work the controls on the console, navigation, sensors. Just stay away from armaments," Captain Paul added with a chuckle. "We aren't going to target the shuttle."

Teddy thought for a moment. He reached over and adjusted his console like he had in VR. He set navigation on the left panel and sensors on the right. He put the shuttle in the center and on the heads up display as well. It was already several hundred miles away. He checked stealth mode, life support, ensured that armaments were secure and then turned to Captain Paul. "I'm ready," he said, not at all sure that he was.

"The ship is yours," Captain Paul said.

"Ship is mine," Teddy replied. Then he took a deep breath and gently squeezed his calves in. The ship slowly moved forward. Teddy studied the readouts on the navigation display. He squeezed harder and leaned forward slightly. The fighter leapt forward, as he felt slight pressure push him back from the inertial dampeners. He was traveling 500 miles per hour. He alternated pressure from one leg to the other and watched as his course changed left and right, his body swaying slightly back and forth."

"Bringing your feet up and down in the stirrups will change your course in three dimensions. If you lift your feet evenly, the fighter will move laterally up or down. If you do it with your heels up or down, then the nose of the fighter will move accordingly," Captain Paul instructed. "That's the only real difference from riding a horse. We have three dimensions here."

Teddy raised his feet slightly in the stirrups and the fighter moved up. He pushed down and it came back down. He moved his heels up and down and the nose of the fighter shifted. It took him a few tries to settle the nose back on the shuttle's course as shown on the navigation and sensor consoles. Teddy veered left, right, up and down  and then leaned back slightly and brought the fighter to a dead stop. The shuttle was now several thousand miles away.

"All the dressage commands are the same?" Teddy asked.

"Basically, yes. Except for up and down, of course."

"Canter, half pass, pirouette?"

"Yes."

Teddy smiled. He kept his right leg in place and slid his left leg back and pressed. The shuttle started to spin in place. He lifted one leg and it started to spin in three dimensions. Inside the fighter he only felt a slight push sideways, while the optical display showed the stars spinning around them. He brought the spin to a halt and realigned the fighter with the shuttle's path. He moved the fighter forward slightly and pressed slightly with his right leg. The fighter drifted to the left. He pushed with his left leg and the fighter drifted right. He leaned back slightly and pressed harder and the fighter drifted backwards. He repeated the maneuvers, drifting left, right, up and down. Smiling even broader, he centered the fighter on the shuttle's path once again.

Captain Paul just sat and watched, quietly pleased at Teddy's progress so far. The fighter was moving forward at a leisurely 450 miles per hour. The shuttle was over 10,000 miles away.

Teddy slid his right leg back for a canter command, leaned forward slightly and squeezed with both legs, subconsciously clicking his tongue as he did. The fighter leaped forward as Teddy laughed out loud. The navigation display no longer read miles-per-hour, now it read miles-per-second, with the number quickly climbing. Eight. Ten. Fifteen. Twenty-five.

"The fighter will keep accelerating as long as

you lean forward until it maxes out," Captain Paul reminded Teddy. "We are in space with negligible friction, so unlike a plane, we can maintain this speed without the need for further thrust."

Teddy slowly sat up. The fighter's acceleration slowed, then stopped, but its speed did not diminish. The sensor console showed the shuttle quickly approaching.

"Please try not to hit my shuttle," Captain Paul said quietly.

Startled, Teddy glanced at the sensor console and then the heads-up display. A collision warning was blinking on the screen. Panicked, Teddy squeezed with his right leg. The fighter veered left. He tried to compensate with his left and the fighter veered right and then went into a spin. He inadvertently lifted one foot and the spin took on another direction, the stars now flying crazily across the display.

"Breathe," Captain Paul said quietly. "Breathe and recover. There is nothing to hit out here but the moon. And we aren't close to it. Not yet, anyway."

Teddy sat up and tried to concentrate. He was starting to get vertigo from the spinning stars. "Turn off visual," he said and the stars were gone. He leaned back and breathed deeply, slowly pushing his leg against the spin. He adjusted his position several times and then turned on the visual again. They were still moving forward at twenty-five miles per second, but they had stopped spinning. That was something near 90,000 miles an hour, Teddy calculated roughly in his head. He did not want to think what the g-forces would have been during that spin without the inertial dampeners.

"Sorry about that spin," Teddy said.

"You forgot you were riding a horse," Captain Paul said. "Stick with your horse training, albeit with some modifications, and you will be fine. Now set a course for the Moon."

"The Moon?"

"Yes. Let's do a loop around the Moon and then head home. And you can pick up the pace a little. I don't want to stay out here all night."

Teddy was more than willing to stay out all night, and the next day for that matter. He never really believed he would fly a spaceship. Even when Chuck stumbled across the Delorian, Teddy wasn't convinced. It was just too unbelievable. And now he was out in space.

"The Moon," Captain Paul interrupted his daydreaming.

Teddy tried to recall the details of the navigation module. How did you calculate all the factors? First you had to establish the Moon's relative position in relation to the fighter's and then you had to factor in their trajectories and mass and...

Teddy had a brain storm. "Al, calculate best course to the Moon."

"Calculated and on display," Al replied. "Recommended adjustments to course noted."

Teddy altered the fighter's direction and increased its speed to match Al's recommended flight path and then glanced at Captain Paul for further comments.

"Lunar One to Lunar Two," Captain Paul said.

"Lunar Two copies."

"Head back to base and park in my usual spot. We are going to take a lap around the block before we head in."

"Roger, Lunar One."

"Lunar Two. Take over Section One in the morning. I think Trainee Watson will need to sleep in."

"Roger, Lunar One. Lunar Two heading back to base."

"I think this just might work," Captain Paul said. "We just have to make sure the others become as comfortable riding a horse as you are. Otherwise, I think we will have to get rid of all the pilots and recruit the University Equestrian Team instead."

Teddy wasn't sure if Captain Paul was joking or not. But what he did understand is that he had made the cut. He would be flying fighters in space.

# CHAPTER NINETEEN

Teddy didn't think he would ever fall asleep that night. Not after flying around the Moon. Only a handful of people had ever done that and it had taken years of training. He had done it on a whim during the night. Captain Paul was right, the Delorian technology was so far beyond Earth's that it was impossible to comprehend.

Captain Paul had Teddy land back in the same field. It was 0430 and Captain Paul's Honda was sitting there waiting for them. Lt. Turner was not there.

"I had Al bring the Honda down here," Captain Paul explained when he saw Teddy looking into the empty car. "That way Lt. Turner could get some sleep. Al also flew the fighter to the field and will fly it back to its base."

Before Captain Paul left Teddy's dorm room, he retrieved the spacesuit and showed Teddy how to contact him on the wrist band they all wore. Teddy lay down, but sleep would not come. Finally, when the sun came up, he managed to fall asleep for a couple of hours. At 1100 he was awake again and figured he might as well get back to work, so he called Captain Paul, who instructed him to take an Uber down to The Barracks. Once there, Captain Paul sat Teddy in the Honda.

"Your wrist bands do not have the surveillance blocking capability that mine has," Captain Paul explained. "You can tell the others about your flight last night, but avoid saying Moon and space. Make it sound like you wre flying an Earth ship, not a spaceship. I'm sure you can figure out how to do it so they understand what you mean."

Teddy could not wait to tell the others. His first chance was at lunch. "Where were you this morning?" Carlos asked when Teddy joined them for lunch. Most of Alpha was sitting in a group in the grass enjoying another catered lunch.

"Yea, Lt. Turner said you were sleeping in," Patrick added.

Teddy looked around to see if any of the UVA students were within earshot. When he saw they were clear he answered. "Captain Paul took me for a test flight last night. We didn't get back until 0400."

"A test flight? In what?"

"In the fighter," Teddy answered.

Carlos looked to see if anyone was listening. "You mean THE fighter," he said in a hushed voice.

"Yes. It was incredible. He piloted it up, but then when we got high, and I mean really high, he turned the controls over to me. It is the sweetest thing I have ever flown. And fast. You don't know the meaning of fast until you have flown it. And nimble. We were all over the sky." He stopped talking when one of the UVA students walked by. When she was out of earshot, he continued.

"Now I know why we are here learning to ride. The flight controls are unlike anything you have ever seen. It is controlled entirely by your legs and seat. It is just like riding a horse."

"Except you don't get bucked off," Patrick joked.

"I don't know," Teddy said. "I screwed up once and we went into an incredible spin. I don't even want to know what the g-forces were."

"A spin can get you killed really fast," Patrick Tanaka said, thinking back to his early jet training. "There's no coming out of it. You just spin till you hit the ground."

"You forget, I was real, real high. Nothing to hit and a long time to recover," Teddy said.

"Oh, that high," Patrick said.

"Yes, much higher than the first check-out ride that we did. Remember the video that Captain Paul showed us of the downed ship?"

"Yes."

"We went there!"

"You went to the …"

"Shhhh," Teddy said quickly.

"You went there?"

"Yes. I flew most of the way and then Captain Paul took the controls and took us down. We hovered not twenty feet over the crash site."

"Wow."

"I'm telling you. It's real. It wasn't a video, or VR, it was real. I don't think I truly believed it until now," Teddy continued.

"Not even after the first intro flight?" Anita Kataja asked. "That did it for me."

"That was amazing," Teddy agreed. "But it was still relatively low. Not as far out as this was."

"I don't know," Carlos said with a smile. "I think the meet and greet Chuck did the other night in the break room convinced me." They all started laughing when they thought back to that night.

"Katie says Chuck's call sign should be 'Squealer,'" Sarah said. They all started laughing again.

Brenda, one of the UVA students walked over to the group with a lunch tray in her hand. "Mind if I join you?"

"Sure," they replied as they made room for her.

"What are you talking about," she asked.

They looked at each other, then Teddy spoke up.

"I was just giving them a motivational speech to encourage them to learn to ride."

"I'll give you one," Brenda said. "Ms. Dawson told us that your Captain Paul has offered her a bonus of $500 for every one of you who passes the riding test at the end of the week and she will divide up the money among all of us. I could really use the money."

"Well, the bonus is in the bag for Teddy here," Carlos said. "He has already qualified."

"Yea, but the rest of you, I don't know," Teddy said with a grin.

"Patrick doesn't have a prayer," Anita said.

"Yea, you ride like a sack of potatoes," Anita chimed in, smiling at Patrick.

"I just do that to make you look good," Patrick responded good naturedly.

"Talking about sack of potatoes, Lt. Turner was the first one to come off. Did you see him? He rolled right off the back of the horse," Carlos said.

"Yes, he might be able to fly a shuttle, but I don't see him qualifying for anything else," Patrick added.

"What's a shuttle?" Brenda asked.

The group got suddenly quiet. "It's a small transport plane," Teddy quickly filled the silence. "Patrick here is trying to get into fighters, so he looks down on those of us who fly closer to the

Earth."

"What do you fly? Brenda asked.

"I fly helicopters for the Coast Guard," Teddy explained. "Search and rescue stuff." The group gave a silent sigh of relief as Teddy steered the conversation to safer ground. Soon they were all talking about what they had been flying before they came to Virginia.

When lunch ended, the trainees went back to learning to ride with new enthusiasm.

# CHAPTER TWENTY

By Tuesday afternoon everyone could sit on a horse with varying degrees of proficiency and had progressed to being allowed to hold the reins, although not without the instructors yelling at them to hold lightly. Several, Lt. Turner included, still rode like a sack of potatoes. When they complained to the instructors about the difficulty of posting, they were told they could sit the trot if they wanted. Depending on the horse, this was even worse than posting as they bounced painfully on the saddle.

Phillip tried to ride a full lap before stopping next to Teddy, who was standing on the edge of the ring. "How do you sit the trot?" Phillip asked. "This is impossible. If I do another lap like that, I will never have children."

"You have to relax into the horse, move with it. Don't tense up."

"Easy for you to say," Phillip complained as he tried to relax his seat.

This conversation was repeated throughout the day as trainees tried to learn to relax. Tuesday evening PT was much slower as little used leg and inner thigh muscles objected to riding horses. On Wednesday morning, most of the trainees were limping. Riding horses was pure torture. That evening, only military discipline got them into PT formation next to the JAG school.

As the trainees began their PT, an Army Blackhawk helicopter landed behind the building. An officer climbed out with an aide and headed for the front door where he was met by a Lieutenant Colonel. They talked for a moment and then headed for the squadron. Lt. Turner was leading the group in jumping jacks when one trainee motioned for him to look behind him. He turned and saw three officers heading towards him, the one in the lead wearing two stars. Lt. Turner called a halt to the PT and came to attention, throwing a crisp salute.

"Who's in charge of this group," the General asked, clearly irate about something.

"That would be Captain Paul, General. He's not here right now," Lt. Turner responded. "However, I can contact him if you want." Lt. Turner was spared having to deal with an irate Major General when he saw Paul's gold Honda pulling up to the front of the JAG school. "Here he is, Sir," he said as he pointed to the Honda.

The General and his entourage headed over to

Captain Paul, while the squadron started doing sit-ups, which allowed them to watch what was going on without being too obvious. Captain Paul walked up to the General and offered his hand to shake.

"Oh, boy," Daniel said to the group. "You see that," he said. "No salute. I knew he wasn't a Captain."

The group continued to surreptitiously watch, although they were too far away to hear what was being said. They saw Captain Paul show the General a document. When the conversation ended, the General saluted Captain Paul, who casually returned the salute. The General then headed back to the waiting helicopter.

"Man, Captain Paul must have some serious juice if a two-star is saluting him," Patrick whispered as he held Alex's feet for sit-ups.

When the Blackhawk flew off, Liam wanted to talk to Paul. But instead, he took the group for a very slow two-mile run. When they returned, he hunted up Paul.

"So, what was that all about?" Liam asked.

"What? TJAG?" Paul asked innocently.

"TJAG?"

"The Judge Advocate General," Paul explained. "He is in charge of the Army JAG Corp and wondered what we were doing here? This is his school after all."

"What did you tell him?"

"I told him the truth," Paul said.

"You told him about the..." Liam paused and glanced at Paul's wrist.

"It's on," Paul said.

"You told him about the Delorians?" Liam asked.

"Okay, I didn't tell him the whole truth," Paul replied. "I told him we were part of a black ops, that these pilots had to learn how to ride horses quickly and his people were being marvelously accommodating to us while we trained."

"What did you show him?"

"Oh, that." Paul laughed. "I have some very official looking top secret documents that are quite impressive. All forgeries, of course. But very good ones. He won't even be able to check their authenticity for fear of violating the orders."

"Delorian forgeries," Liam said.

"Naturally. The very best. They have the DOD computers create the orders. Can't get any better than that."

Liam wondered what logistics Paul had to do to run the training and was glad that all he had to do was take care of the trainees. He was having enough trouble doing that while trying to learn to ride.

Thursday morning the trainees were still pretty

sore as they climbed aboard the charter bus. Even the section leaders, who had ridden before, were feeling it as they had not ridden recently. Captain Paul met the bus at the barn. After asking the driver to step out for a moment, he closed the door and addressed the group.

"I know you are all pretty sore right now. But you are on the back side now. In a day or two you will actually want to live again." The group chuckled. Some groaned. "But let me put this in perspective, to remind you what we are doing. It is imperative that you can isolate your muscles so you can be doing one thing with your hands, while doing something completely different with each of your legs and your seat. That is exactly what you will be doing today on the horses. Relax. Do not be stiff. You want to be the horse. You want to get where you don't even have to think about what you are asking, you just do it. It will be the same in the fighters. Flying them will have to become second nature, because you will be too busy trying to stay alive to think about flying."

Captain Paul paused as he surveyed the trainees. "I took a week-long polo clinic here years ago. And it was the same way. On Wednesday, I was too sore to walk. On Thursday things started to come together and on Saturday I had it. I didn't even think about the horse anymore, I was too focused on hitting the ball. That is where you need to be. You need to be able to think about what you want to do, or I should say, where you want to go, and not have to think about how to do it." He paused to let his words soak in. "Okay folks, you got this." He opened the bus door and everyone filed out.

* * *

This was actually starting to get a little easier, Liam thought as the day progressed. He had started out on a lunge line in a twenty-meter circle. The UVA student stood in the middle, holding the lunge line, while Liam's horse walked and trotted around her. Liam was allowed to use the stirrups, but not his hands.

As the horse trotted, Liam had to put his hands on his head, shoulders, knees and toes, all without falling off. It was to give him balance and allow him to move his upper body, while his legs worked independently. And, rather than the UVA student controlling the horse like she had done earlier in the week, he was supposed to make the horse walk, trot, canter and then slow down, all by using his legs and his seat. Liam managed to get the horse to move forward at a walk and trot on command, but never could get the horse to slow down without using the reins.

After that, Liam was put in an arena and told to move the horse in circles, figure eights and around the ring, while holding his hands still. On Tuesday, this had been an impossibility. Today he was starting to get it, although there was still a lot of miscommunications between him and his horse.

Near the end of this session, he pressed his right leg against the girth and the horse moved sideways across the arena. He pushed his left leg against the girth and the horse moved back. That was it! He got it, he thought, as his horse obediently moved sideways back across the arena.

He looked around. No one was watching. Even the UVA student was working with someone else. He felt like there should be fanfare, a band even. He rode over to the side of the arena and climbed off his horse, his legs still protesting. For the first time he thought he might be able to do this.

At lunch time Liam wanted to stand up and announce that he got it. He was sitting on the grass eating a ham sandwich when he heard a commotion over by one arena. Idly, he picked up his plate and sandwich and walked over. Several UVA students were setting up a number of jumps, adjusting horizontal poles at various heights. Another student was riding a horse around the ring. When the students moved to the side, the horse broke into a canter and started headed for the first jump. The horse cleared it easily and turned for the next jump.

"That's a seven-jump course," Liam heard Donna Peterson explain to someone next to her. "The trick is to keep the horse calm between the jumps and not have them get too excited and rush."

Liam watched. Although at a canter, the horse was clearly relaxed, with the horse twisting and turning easily through the course. When it was over, the crowd of spectators cheered. The rider brought the horse to a stop and patted its neck enthusiastically.

"What's the big deal? She's using reins," someone from the crowd said. Liam looked over to see who the speaker was. Naturally, it was Chuck Williams. He wondered if the Delorians made a mistake including him in the group. He seemed to be nothing but trouble.

The rider heard the comment as she looked over at the crowd. She leaned down and spoke to one of the UVA students. A moment later the student reached up and pulled the bridal off the horse's head. The crowd went silent as the rider sat up and the horse started trotting, before breaking into a slow canter. The horse and rider did a complete lap around the arena at a canter and then the rider pointed the horse at the first jump.

Liam found he was holding his breath as the horse approached the jump. It had to be a three-feet high. The horse cleared it effortlessly, and the rider stayed on. Liam knew that you did not hold onto a horse with the reins, but seeing someone jump without reins was mind boggling.

He watched as the horse completed the entire course at a canter and then stopped near the watching UVA students.

"Yep, no big deal," Liam heard Donna Peterson say to Chuck as the crowd cheered. The rider slid off the horse and patted it again as one of the UVA students put its bridle back on. The rider pulled off her helmet as she walked towards the crowd. It was Catherine Miller!

"She shouldn't have any trouble flying the fighter," a familiar voice said. Liam turned and saw Paul standing next to him.

"How did she do that?" Liam asked. "No reins."

"I keep telling you," Paul said. "Reins are not the most important control. The seat and legs are crucial. Here and in the fighter. However, it takes a very well-trained horse and rider to do what you just saw."

"Did you know she was going to jump?" Liam asked, both amazed and terrified that Paul may now ask him to jump.

"I knew when I saw them putting a jump saddle on the horse," Paul said.

"There are different types of saddles?"

"Of course," Paul said as he walked over to congratulate Catherine on her ride.

Liam shook his head. And here he thought he had accomplished something when he got his horse to move sideways.

# CHAPTER TWENTY-ONE

Thursday's training was wrapping up and the trainees were wandering over to the bus. The section leaders reported to Lt. Turner when their section was all present. When Chuck Williams had not boarded the bus, Lt. Turner sent Donna Peterson to look for him. She returned a few minutes later, looking madder than hell with Chuck Williams in tow.

That evening after PT and dinner, Katie, Brenda, Karen and Donna were sharing a table in the O-Club at the top floor of the JAG School, enjoying a nightcap before going to bed.

"What happened with you and Chuck Williams?" Katie asked Donna. "You looked like you wanted to kill him."

"First, he does not make it to the bus on time so I get called out in front of everyone to go look for him. And then I find him in the barn trying to hit on one of the UVA students," Donna complained.

"Hit on. What do you mean by that?" Katie asked.

"Oh, he was doing that 'I'm a fighter pilot, so I'm sexy,' crap. You know, his usual sleazy self."

"The UVA students are adults," Brenda said. "They are all at least twenty, if not older."

"That's not the point," Donna said. "He needs to focus. He could at least make it to the bus on time. Instead, he chases anything in a skirt."

"He hit on me last week," Karen interjected.

The others turned and looked at her. "Really? What did you do?" Katie asked.

"Shot him down," Karen said, pantomiming a plane crashing with her hand. "Wasn't too difficult. He does understand no."

"He tried to slime me at the O-Club on Monday," Katie said. "But I shot him down before he even got off the ground. That's what you have to do, a pre-emptive strike."

The ladies laughed.

"Why is it that the ones you are not interested in are chasing after you and the ones you are interested in are not available?" Karen asked, a bit too seriously.

"That is called the universe not being fair," Brenda chimed in. "Who is it you are interested in? Heh?" She asked Karen.

"I bet it is Carlos," Donna guessed. "Those big brown eyes of his. Funny, witty, and not so full of himself."

"Well, I can tell who Donna is interested in," Brenda said with a laugh. "Maybe you should just let that blonde hair of yours down and go flash your baby blues at him. He won't last a second after that."

"I don't think that will work," Katie said when it appeared the Donna was considering the suggestion.

"Why not?" Brenda challenged. "Look at her. Do you think any guy has a chance against her?"

"He was with someone Tuesday night," Katie said.

"How do you know?" Donna asked.

"I have the room next to his and I heard them."

"Who was it?"

"The walls are not that thin. I couldn't tell."

"I bet it was Sarah. But, so what?" Brenda said, undeterred. "That was Tuesday. Ancient history. You want him girl, you go for him."

"It wasn't a girl," Katie said.

"What?" Brenda asked.

"Tuesday night. All I could tell is that it wasn't a girl," Katie repeated.

"Oh, Damn," Brenda said, and then turned to

Donna. "See, I told you. The universe is just not fair."

The ladies nodded in agreement as they sipped their drinks.

"I think it's Daniel," Katie broke the silence. "I saw Karen talking with him at lunch," Katie informed the group.

"Listen to you. Can't talk to anyone without it being a flirtation," Karen replied.

"So, who is it? Come on, girl, give," Brenda said.

I've been eyeing Teddy Watson," Karen confessed after taking another sip of her drink.

"Forget it," Donna said. "You don't have a chance with him."

"What do you mean?" Karen asked.

"He was an equestrian through high school and college," Donna replied with a tone that meant it was self-evident.

"So?"

"So, he is gay," Donna said.

"Not him, too. How do you know?" Karen asked.

"All equestrian guys are gay," Donna pronounced.

"I beg to differ with you on that," Katie interrupted. "I have known a fair number of cowboys and I know they were not gay."

"You need to look somewhere else, girlfriend,"

Donna said.

"It's not like we will have time to date anyone anyway," Brenda complained. "Not with our training schedule."

"I think that's why Chuck is pushing so hard," Donna said.

"Well, good luck with that. If he's my only choice, I'll just stick to the training," Karen said.

They raised their glasses in a silent toast as the conversation drifted to other topics before they called it a night.

Karen finished her beer and headed downstairs. She paused at her room, before going down the hall and knocking on a door near the end.

"Mind if I come in for a minute?" she asked when the door opened. She walked in, noting he was only wearing a pair of boxers. She had not really planned on coming here, but the earlier conversation about having no time to socialize had made her think. Now she did not know what to say.

"Donna told me you were gay," she blurted out.

"She did? Why did she do that?" Teddy asked.

"Something about you riding dressage through school. She said all those guys were gay."

"That is such a stereotype," Teddy said.

"A lot of stereotypes are true," Karen said.

"So, you want to know if I am gay?" Teddy

asked.

Karen ran her hands across his bare chest. "I want you to tell me you are not."

"You want me to prove it?" Teddy asked with a laugh.

"I think you just did," Karen said as she wrapped her arms around him.

In another dorm room down the hall Carlos was lying on his back in bed. "I probably should get back to my room," Carlos said, although he made no attempt to reach for his clothes.

"Stay. There is nothing wrong with you being here. It's not fraternization. We're not even in the same branch. You're Coast Guard and I'm Navy. And the Captain said we are all trainees, so you don't outrank me here.

"So, I can't order you to do anything?" Carlos asked with feigned innocence.

"You can't order, but you can certainly try to convince me," Alex replied with a grin.

# CHAPTER TWENTY-TWO

Saturday morning finally arrived. Test day. The trainees were still sore, but they could walk. They were allowed to choose their favorite horse and practice with the UVA students in the outside rings. When they felt they were ready, they would enter the indoor arena, where Captain Paul and Julie Dawson were sitting in the judging booth. Each had to complete a basic dressage test, similar to the one they had seen the first day. First they would walk, trot and canter around the ring and then in 20-meter circles, all while using their reins. Then they would have to do it with the reins lying on the horse's neck.

The section leaders went first and passed without difficulty. Then other trainees filtered in. Those who did not pass, were allowed to go outside and practice some more before coming in for a retest.

Liam felt sick with stress. He didn't want to let Paul down, he was the XO, and he really wanted to fly the fighter. Why did it have to be so complicated? Why couldn't it be like a normal aircraft? But it wasn't, it was a spaceship.

Liam entered the ring. He was on Blaze, which was the horse he had ridden on Thursday. They walked to the center of the ring and he nodded to the judges. He then walked, trotted and cantered, while using the reins. He had this part. The horse even changed his gaits within a pace or two from where he gave the command. And then he came to the part where he had to do the half pass. He took the turn and headed down one side of the arena. He pressed the horse's outer flank with his leg and the horse moved sideways. When he had crossed the width of the arena, he put pressure with the other leg and the horse drifted back. Liam realized that he was holding his breath and had to breathe before he passed out. Another circle and he brought the horse to a stop in the middle of the arena.

This was the tough part. He leaned over and tied the reins over the horse's neck. He saw Paul nod to him, a slight smile on his face. He had to peg this. He sat up on his saddle and took a deep breath before squeezing gently with both legs. His horse moved forward at a walk. He approached the wall and asked for the horse to turn left by pressing with his outside leg. Blaze complied. Liam hoped it was at his command and not just to avoid running into the wall.

He squeezed harder and the horse trotted. At the end of the arena the horse turned, but there was a wall there, so that was no big deal. Now he had to make the horse come off the wall and do a circle. He squeezed his outside leg again. Nothing. He squeezed again and pressed in slightly with his inner leg. He leaned slightly inward, willing the horse to turn. Much to Liam's relief, Blaze finally responded, although his 20-meter circle looked more like an abstract polygon. After that the half pass was easy.

The last part of the test was trotting up the center of the arena and stopping the horse without using reins. He turned to go up the center of the arena. Blaze turned and proceeded up somewhere near the center of the ring. Liam sat back and tried to sink into the saddle, whispering whoa, under his breath. He had only managed to do this once before. He passed the center and kept going. He sat harder and leaned back slightly, trying not to bounce in the saddle. Blaze finally stopped about twenty feet from the end of the arena. Liam leaned forward and patted Blaze's neck, before looking up at Paul.

"Not the prettiest performance I have ever seen, but I think that will do for now," Paul said.

Liam breathed a sigh of relief, untied the reins, and rode out to give the horse to someone else.

By noon all the trainees had taken the test, some several times.

At 1300 hours, everyone met at the grassy area outside the barn for lunch, which was being catered by a bar-b-que truck. Soon the smell of bar-b-qued ribs wafted across the grounds as the trainees mixed with the UVA students. Captain Paul strode in front of the group.

"Let me divert your attention from your food for a second," Captain Paul said. "A week ago, I contacted Ms. Dawson and presented her with an impossible task. I needed her to teach 31 aviators how to ride in one week. She laughed at me, until she realized I was serious. And here we are one week later and I have 31 very sore pilots." Laughter rippled across the crowd. "I think we should give Ms. Dawson and all of her students a round of applause for their herculean efforts in torturing you this week." Cheers rose from the assembled aviators.

When the applause died down, Captain Paul continued. "Although I would not want to see your dressage scores, you all demonstrated that you grasped the basics, that you could in fact use your arms, legs and seat independently. And most of you eventually got your horses to move in the right direction without reins. Stopping was a bit of a problem for most of you, but then again aviators are not known for stopping." Another round of laughter. So, in light of my agreement, I will be presenting Ms. Dawson and her wonderful staff with a bonus of $15,500 for their efforts." There was another round of applause, this time joined by the UVA students.

"Now I want you all to relax and enjoy your food. Our flight does not leave until 1800 hours."

# CHAPTER TWENTY-THREE

Sunday morning the trainees were back at their base in the abandoned hangar. After lunch on Saturday, they had taken their charter bus back to the JAG school, and packed their belongings before being driven to the Charlottesville airport. There, another C-130 was waiting for them.

"Got to love the Gulf Coast," Carlos complained to the group as they lined up for morning PT on the old tarmac. "Six a.m. and it's already 80 degrees, with 100% humidity."

"So glad we are not back in Virginia with no humidity and 70 degrees. That would be horrible," Alex joked back.

They continued to complain as they jogged around the perimeter of the abandoned airfield.

After showers and breakfast, Lt. Turner led the group back into the classroom. At the front of the room were thirty-one containers of VR equipment.

Lt. Turner walked to the front of the room. "I need you all to grab these chairs and move them to the sides of the room. We need as much empty space as possible." When they had dragged the reclining chairs to the sides of the room, Lt. Turner led them back into the hangar where a Conex storage container sat in the otherwise empty building. He opened the back of the container and turned to the group.

"Each of you take one of the boxes in here and set it up in the classroom," Lt. Turner instructed.

The trainees pulled boxes out of the Conex. The boxes were three feet long and about two feet wide and deep. Although large, they were not that heavy.

"What is this?" someone asked as they started opening their box in the classroom.

"It's got legs," someone else answered.

Lt. Turner already knew what was in the boxes, but he waited to let the trainees figure it out. He watched as they pulled out a molded plastic object about two feet long and fifteen inches wide and just as high. The top sloped down and then back up. There were also four screw in legs in the box.

"I still don't know what this is," Chuck said as he finished screwing in the legs and standing it up. It stood about three feet high.

"Oh, no. It isn't," Katie said.

"Yes, it is," Brenda responded.

"What is it," Chuck asked.

"It's a saddle stand," Katie said.

A groan went through the group.

"There are also saddles in the container," Lt. Turner said. "Go get a saddle and set it up on your stand."

The trainees complained as they went back to the Conex and found the saddles and set them up on the stands. The complaints died quickly when Captain Paul walked into the classroom.

"I see you have found your new toys," Captain Paul said to the group. Adjust the saddle and the stirrups on the stands and have a seat." He waited until everyone was sitting on their saddle.

"I'm still sore from last week," Daniel complained as he sat down.

"These things move," Chuck said as he rocked back and forth.

"They do, although not a lot," Captain Paul said. "These are dynamic saddle stands. They are designed so someone trying out a new saddle can move around to see how the saddle fits them. We will use them for a different purpose."

"Although most of you are not ready for a real dressage test, I believe you now understand the basics. However, we need to hone your skills before we can put most of you in a fighter. This stand will allow you to practice those skills without worrying about falling off your horse or getting beat to death sitting a trot."

"I want all of you to take a minute or two to move around on that stand. Get comfortable with it and figure out how much you can move without falling off. Anyone falling off owes me a drink." Captain Paul waited while everyone rocked back and forth and side to side. There was not much movement to the stand, just enough to give you an idea of how your body would shift on the saddle.

"Now try it with your eyes closed," Captain Paul said after a couple minutes.

After a couple more minutes, he got their attention again. "Good, no one got thrown. Now come on up here and get your VR equipment. You can take any container, your A.I. will find you when you log in." As the trainees came up to grab a VR container, Captain Paul continued. "You will find there is a new piece of equipment in the containers. They replace the booties you used before. They go over your legs. You will need to put them on under your flight suits. You can leave your underwear on."

The trainees pulled out the goggles and gloves and then pulled out leggings.

"These are pantyhose," Chuck said shocked, holding up a pair of leggings that did indeed look like a pair of shear pantyhose.

"What's the problem?" Brenda deadpanned.

"Not your color?"

"No," Donna chimed in, "he wears the black ones with the lace."

The trainees looked around uncomfortably, before reluctantly taking off their boots and flight suits so they could put on the leggings.

"Shouldn't there be music on?" someone quipped from the back.

The leggings slipped on a lot like the Delorian spacesuit. When the trainees had finished dressing, Captain Paul instructed them to climb back on their saddles and put on the VR goggles. The goggles were still clear so they could see Captain Paul at the front of the room.

"Maybe you won't get bucked off this horse," Daniel teased Jeffrey as they climbed onto the saddles.

Jeffrey was about to respond when suddenly he found himself sitting on a horse in an open field. Glancing around, he saw all the other trainees were also sitting on horses around him. Captain Paul was sitting on a horse in front. Despite the distance, he could hear Captain Paul perfectly.

"Now we are going to refine your skills. Since you don't have to worry about getting bucked off or trying to sit a trot, we will fine tune your leg and seat commands. Your A.I.'s will walk you through the specific training each of you needs. When you have mastered it on your virtual horse, you will move on to VR training for the fighter. The 'pantyhose' you are wearing will map all of your movements. Any questions?"

When there were none, the scene suddenly changed so most trainees were sitting alone on their horse, while their A.I. spoke commands in their ear. Katie, Donna, Teddy and Catherine found themselves in Delorian fighters.

# CHAPTER TWENTY-FOUR

Liam found himself on his virtual horse in a field with forty or fifty other riders. The riders were all formally dressed with knee-high black boots, white or tan pants and jackets. Most riders wore black jackets, although some wore red. All had black helmets and many were carrying short hunt whips.

Liam recognized the scene. The sound of a hunt horn filled the air and a pack of thirty or so hounds bounded across the field, accompanied by a huntsman and a couple of whips, all wearing traditional red jackets.

"Paul thought you would enjoy this, so we have special training set for you today," Al said.

"Really? A fox hunt?" Liam asked.

"Yes. It is perfect. We will start with riding out into the woods with the hounds. You will have to control your horse's speed and direction with your seat. You will have reins for the simulation, but they will not control the horse, no matter what you do with them. Your mission is to stay with the pack of riders. Don't run into them, don't lose them, don't pass them."

"That seems simple enough," Liam said. No sooner had he said that than the huntsman blew his hunt horn and led the pack of hounds across an open field. The rest of the riders followed, with the riders wearing red coats leading and those wearing black coats in the rear.

Grabbing his reins, Liam tried to pull his horse around to follow the departing group. Nothing happened. He yanked on the reins again before remembering Al's instructions. Putting the reins down, Liam pressed the horses flank with his right leg. The horse turned left. Liam squeezed with both legs and the horse trotted forward.

Liam started to overtake the horse in front of him and barely remembered to sit back into the saddle in time to avoid riding into him. Liam rode in the back of the group, practicing his commands. Side to side was relatively easy, as was speeding up. Slowing and stopping were much more difficult. He had plenty of time to practice as the hunt field would slow and stop while the hounds were cast to search for scent and then moved on to the next covert to try again.

As Liam got comfortable with these moves, the hunt sped up. A cry went up from the hounds and they were off, running across another field and into the woods. The horses ran single file through a trail. But unlike a real hunt where you could expect your horse to follow the one in front of it, Liam had to direct his horse on each turn. He discovered this when he got to the first turn and his horse ran straight into the woods when he did not give the correct leg command.

"I told you," Al said. "You have to instruct your horse to turn. Otherwise, it will run into a tree."

"At least it was not a real tree," Liam said as he directed his horse out of the woods at a walk and then started trotting, then cantering down the trail to catch up with the hunt.

Soon Liam was in a fast canter, steering his horse with his legs and leaning slightly side to side as the trail veered back and forth. Not having to worry about posting, falling off his horse or how much it would hurt if he hit a tree, made the exercise enjoyable. Soon he had caught up with the hunt and was able to keep up with them, although slowing down when they did continued to be a problem.

Finally, the hunt ended when the fox went to ground and the hounds milled around the fox's den, marking it. The huntsman counted the hounds, before leading the pack back to the kennels, with the rest of the hunt following. Liam followed the hunt, easily following at a walk and slow trot. Al took this opportunity to critique his performance, often showing Liam what he done in a hologram that floated unnoticed above the other rider's heads. The VR program ended when the hunt arrived at the stables. Liam was now back in the classroom with everyone else. Some of the trainees were climbing off their saddles, while others were still in VR.

"That was a lot easier than real horses," Patrick said as he stretched his legs.

"We should have started with the VR," Chuck said.

"And miss out on Virginia?" Carlos asked. "No way, that was great." He glanced over at Alex.

"The food was pretty good," Chuck agreed.

When everyone had finished VR, Lt. Turner instructed the trainees to dress for PT. After PT and a shower, Liam headed to the breakroom for lunch, but before he got there Paul intercepted him and led him out to the deserted tarmac.

"How did you like the fox hunt?" Paul asked.

"It was interesting," Liam said. "Actually, quite fun."

"I was monitoring you," Paul said. "You improved dramatically as the hunt progressed."

"It helps when you don't have to worry about getting bounced off your horse or running into a tree," Liam explained.

"True," Paul agreed. "However, I think it also

helped when the hunt got exciting. You got into it and started to react by reflex, rather than planning your moves. You started concentrating on the hunt, rather than your horse. It's the same in polo. Once the game starts, you don't even know you are on a horse anymore, all you think about is hitting the ball. That is what you will want to do with the fighter. You want to concentrate on fighting the fighter, not thinking about how to fly it."

"I have a question," Liam asked. "I understand why you are doing the horse training, but why in Virginia on real horses? Why not just do it all on VR? It's much easier, you don't have to worry about falling off."

Paul laughed. "Still upset about falling off?"

"I rather fall off in VR," Liam admitted.

"That is the point," Paul said. "I wanted you to be concerned about falling off. I wanted you to be preoccupied. That way you are not just concentrating on your legs, you have to divide your attention while being stressed. I'm hoping that gives you all an edge in VR and speeds up the learning curve."

"Riding real horses gave me a real incentive to get it right," Liam admitted.

"Do a couple more VR hunts," Paul said. "You keep improving like you are and you will be ready to move to the fighter very soon."

# CHAPTER TWENTY-FIVE

True to Paul's prediction, Liam found himself in a VR Delorian fighter two days later. He was the fourth trainee to progress to fighters after the three section leaders and Catherine. The other three were Patrick Tanaka, Brenda Donaldson, and William Wetherford.

"Welcome to the Delorian fighter," Al said as Liam donned the VR goggles. "Or should I say, welcome to the VR fighter, since you already have flown the real fighter."

"I may have piloted it," Liam responded. "But not well. That's why Paul changed the training program and put us on horses."

"That may be," Al responded. "But the point is that you are here. Now the difference with VR is that we cannot duplicate the forces you will feel when the inertial dampeners are turned down. That is an integral portion of flying you can only obtain when flying the actual fighter. But first you must be comfortable with the controls. Paul asked me to run you through the fighter version of a fox hunt, since you did so well in that scenario earlier. He thinks that will hone your skills so you can progress to the real fighter."

"And just what is the fighter version of fox hunting?" Liam asked.

Suddenly, Liam was in a Delorian fighter somewhere in space. The scene was frozen as he gazed out the front display. Numerous asteroids dotted his view. In the distance Liam saw a boxy looking Red Force fighter, the same one that had attacked him months ago.

"This," Al said, "is the fighter version of fox hunting. Your mission is to destroy the opposing force, or OPFOR as you military types like to call it. It will be attempting to elude you by flying through this asteroid field. Consider the asteroids your path through the forest and the OPFOR is the fox."

"Do I get to say, 'Tally Ho?'" Liam asked.

"If you wish," Al responded. A hunt horn sounded and the program started, with the OPFOR disappearing behind an asteroid.

"Funny," Liam said, as he moved one leg back before squeezing with his calves. The fighter leapt forward. Asteroids careened towards him and soon he was twisting and turning to avoid them. As he did, his hands moved around the console as he activated his shields and sensors and reconfigured the panel so the display was more comfortable for him. He grazed a small boulder and spun out, his shields saving him from obliteration.

He recovered from the spin and adjusted his course to the bearing he thought the OPFOR was heading. He shot past an asteroid just in time to see the OPFOR slip behind another. Increasing his forward shields, he plotted a trajectory the opposite way around the asteroid and came head on with the OPFOR fighter. He barely squeezed off a shot before he was past. He missed and the OPFOR was now on his tail. Suddenly he was the fox.

He squeezed his legs and leaned forward and his fighter leapt again. He spun around one asteroid and headed for another as laser fire shot past him, one beam grazing his rear shield. Belatedly, he remembered to adjust the power to the rear shields, although he left enough to the forward shields to deflect space debris. At least he hoped it was enough. He passed the next asteroid and was in the clear. This was not good. He might be able to outrun the OPFOR, but he could not outrun a laser.

The point was reinforced when his rear shields took a direct hit, taking their power down to 30%. Another hit like that and he would be toast. Then he remembered Paul's demonstration. Leaning back, he spun the fighter 180 degrees and leaned forward. He closed the distance with the OPFOR in seconds and opened fire. The OPFOR exploded in a very satisfactory manner.

Then his ship exploded.

"What? He couldn't have shot me down. I killed him first," Liam objected as he found himself back in the ready room. The Commander on the stage faced him soberly. "Welcome to the afterlife," he said.

"I know, I know," Liam responded impatiently. "This is not fair. I killed him."

"You did," the Commander responded. "And then you killed yourself."

"What? How?"

A hologram appeared above the stage showing the final moments of the battle. Liam watched as he shot the OPFOR and it exploded.

"Yes," he said. "See, I killed him."

"You did," the Commander responded as the hologram continued. "Then you ran your fighter through the expanding debris cloud at 23 miles per second with minimal forward shields. That is how you killed yourself."

Liam watched as the program slowed, showing his fighter hitting the debris field, the shields failing and the fighter disintegrating, all in milliseconds.

"Okay," Liam acknowledged. "Point taken. Now let me do it again."

The program restarted. Once again, the asteroids appeared with the OPFOR in the distance. A hunt horn sounded and the program began. This time the OPFOR took another route through the asteroid field.

"This will be more of a fox hunt than a coyote run," Al said as Liam shot after the OPFOR.

"What are you talking about," Liam said as he swerved around a small asteroid, only to see two more blocking his way. He pulled up, narrowly avoiding them.

"Good 3-dimensional thinking," Al said before answering Liam's question. "A fox hunt tends to stay in one general area with the fox often doubling back on its path. A lot of twisting and turning. A coyote run tends to be straighter and fast. Basically, a very long run."

"So, we are chasing a fox," Liam said as he moved the fighter laterally to avoid another asteroid.

"Exactly," Al said. The next time the OPFOR became visible in the distance, it looked like a cartoon fox.

"Okay," Liam said. "That is too much. Turn it back into the fighter."

The fox turned back into the Red Force fighter before disappearing behind another clump of asteroids. The asteroid debris field was becoming denser and more small pieces began hitting the fighter's shields.

"Shields are degrading," Al warned as lights flashed on the console.

Liam considered for just a second before responding. "Drop stealth mode, divert more power to shields."

He dropped under two asteroids, swung to the left of another and then grazed another, threatening to throw him into a spin and degrading his shields down to 23%. He spotted an opening and shot through it, finding himself in a relatively clear space. Clear, except for three OPFOR fighters, which immediately targeted him.

"Oh, sh…" Liam said as he fired off a wild shot before spinning his fighter and heading back to the relative safety of the asteroid field. Once again, he was the fox. Now he had three OPFORs chasing after him, weapons blazing. Small asteroids around him exploded as they were hit by OPFOR weapons' fire. Liam had to increase his speed to something above reckless as he desperately weaved his way through the asteroid field, trying to avoid enemy fire.

He needed to engage the OPFOR forces, but right now he was too intent on getting out of their sights. If he reversed course like he had done before, he could probably destroy one OPFOR, but the other two would light him up before he could get away. A blast hit his rear shield, taking it down. He had to think of something as his current plan would not last long.

As if on cue, his ship exploded and he was once again sitting in the virtual ready room.

"Welcome to the afterlife," the virtual Commander said.

"This is not the afterlife, this is hell," Liam muttered. "All right, how did I die this time?"

A hologram appeared and Liam watched the last twenty seconds of his flight. He was evading the OPFOR fire, veered around two asteroids, took a blast to the rear shield and then as he was analyzing his shield's power requirements, he smacked right into an asteroid the size of his ship.

"Oh," Liam said, more to himself. "Did not see that one."

"Situational awareness," the Commander started. "How many times do we have to stress situational awareness. You have to pay attention to everything..."

"Oh, shut up," Liam said in disgust. The Commander froze in mid-sentence. Liam almost panicked when he realized that he had said that out loud and then relaxed when he remembered this was VR. "I would have liked to have said that to a few of my flight instructors," he said.

The Commander disappeared, although Liam

remained in the ready room. "You actually did quite well," Al said as a hologram of Liam's fighter appeared in the air over the now deserted stage. "Watch how you progressed." Al narrated as Liam watched his flight through the asteroids. Liam cringed as he grazed one of the asteroids. "In the real world your fighter would have been destroyed that time," Al said. "But I wanted to keep the simulation going."

"Oh, great," Liam muttered. "I was actually worse than I thought I was."

"Are you always a glass half empty guy?" Al asked.

"I died," Liam said. "Repeatedly."

"You are allowed to die in VR. In fact, it is expected. You are learning."

"I am learning how to die," Liam said.

"Okay. Stop it," Al said abruptly. "This is not a pity party. Now grow up and listen." Liam was shocked by the tone, but it did cause him to pay attention. The hologram changed to Liam in a fighter with Paul sitting next to him. "This was your first actual flight in the fighter," Al explained. "Watch your limited ability to control the craft." The visual went into fast-forward as Liam could only marginally control the craft. "Now watch your first VR flight." Again, the view fast-forwarded. "Now watch the progress you have made today," Al said, as today's VR flight played out. "Watch how you are able to control the fighter." Liam watched as the fighter dodged and swerved in an out of the asteroid field until it was finally destroyed.

"But I failed," Liam said.

"Of course, you did," Al replied. "This program is designed to keep getting more difficult until you fail. It is pushing you to failure each time to increase your abilities, much like weight-lifting."

"Oh," Liam said. "But what happens when I get into a real asteroid field?"

Al actually laughed. "There isn't one," he replied. "Not in this solar system. What you flew through in VR is straight out of Star Wars."

"Yes, there is," Liam objected. "There is an asteroid belt out there. I've heard about it."

"You are right," Al agreed. "There is what you call an asteroid belt between Mars and Jupiter and spans an area of roughly 140 million miles."

"Yes. I knew it," Liam said.

"And the average distance between the asteroids is roughly 600,000 miles," Al continued.

"600,000 miles?"

"Yes. The odds of hitting one of them is minuscule."

"So, what we did in VR…"

"Was a VR version of space fox-hunting solely to divert your attention so you could learn to fly the fighter by reflex."

"Oh," Liam said. "It was quite a good program."

"Thank-you," Al said. "Now we have time for one more short run before lunch."

# CHAPTER TWENTY-SIX

As Liam was heading for the breakroom after PT, Captain Paul called out to him. "Lt. Turner, a word please."

"Yes, Sir," Lt. Turner replied. He followed Paul through the hangar and out the front door onto the tarmac where they were alone.

"Al sent me the link to your session this morning. Seems like you had a very interesting time of it," Paul said as they walked out on the tarmac.

"Oh, yes, Sir," Liam kept it formal as he believed Paul was about to dress him down for his spat with Al. "I'm sorry, Sir. I was just getting very frustrated, and then Al jumped all over me. He sounded just like my father."

"What are you talking about?" Paul asked.

"When Al dressed me down," Liam said.

"Oh, that," Paul said. "I saw that, but that's not what I'm here about. I watched your flying. Al was right, you have really progressed. And doing it in a fox hunt was a stroke of genius."

"If you do say yourself," Liam added.

"What? Oh, that was not my idea," Paul said. "That was Al."

"Al came up with the fox hunt?" Liam asked. "I was sure you had."

"No, that was all Al. Although, I think that was a very good idea. I liked the hunt horn."

Liam paused for a moment before responding. "You know, talking to Al is like talking to another person. He's so, so real. It's hard to consider him a computer."

"Then don't," Paul said. "I don't. Treat him like a person. A very smart person. I wasn't kidding when I said I believe he is sentient."

"I can see why," Liam said.

"But that's not the reason I wanted to talk to you," Paul said. "I wondered if you would like to take another spin in the fighter. The real one, not the VR one."

"Hell, yes," Liam said, and then caught himself. "Yes, Sir."

"You don't need to do the 'Sir' stuff when we are alone, Liam," Paul said. "That's just for the trainees. Have to keep up the chain of command."

"When do you want to do it? Tonight?" Liam asked.

"I thought we would go right after lunch," Paul

said. "We don't have to wait for nightfall. We do have stealth mode."

"That will work," Liam said excitedly.

"Have section one's leader take over the squadron for the afternoon session. He can do that. We should be back before supper. Now go get some lunch and then we will take a fighter for a spin."

Liam started heading back to the hangar when Paul called after him. "Actually, I have a better idea," Paul said. "Have the trainees meet in the hangar at 1330 hours. Don't tell them why. We'll give them a surprise demonstration."

At 1330, the trainees were milling around in the hangar. When Captain Paul walked into the hangar, section leader Teddy Watson called everyone to attention. Lt. Turner was not present.

"As you were, Captain Paul said. "Section Leader Watson," Captain Paul said.

"Yes, Sir," Teddy responded.

"Have your people open these doors," Captain Paul said, pointing to the giant hangar doors. "I need a fifty-foot opening."

Teddy sent his section to the center of the doors, hoping they could open the huge hangar doors, particularly since they probably had not been used since World War II. Surprisingly, the doors opened smoothly, like they had been recently serviced. When the doors were open fifty feet, Captain Paul had all the trainees move over to the side wall.

"Do you think he's bringing a fighter in?" Jeffrey whispered to Daniel, who was standing next to him.

"In the middle of the day?" Daniel whispered back.

"They do have stealth mode," Jeffrey said.

"Could be the shuttle," Phillip, who was standing next to them, said.

"No," Jeffrey disagreed. "He comes and goes with the shuttle all the time and doesn't do anything like this. It has to be a fighter."

"Look at this," Alex said. He was wearing his flight suit with the sleeves pushed up to his elbows. The hairs on his arm were standing straight up. There was a subtle hum in the air.

"Close the doors," Captain Paul called out. Section one pushed the giant hangar doors closed. "Lights on," Captain Paul said and the hangar lights came on, illuminating the entire hangar. It was empty. "Stealth off."

A Delorian fighter materialized, parked in the middle of the hangar, sitting on its four landing struts. Although most of the trainees expected something like this, they were still shocked as it suddenly appeared. "Lt. Turner and I are going to take this baby out for a spin in a few minutes. But I thought you might like to see a real Delorian fighter, rather than the VR version," Captain Paul told the assembled trainees. "Take a few minutes to look her over while I get my flight suit on. Just don't hurt the paint job." With that, he headed for the dorm room, while the trainees went over to the fighter and inspected it. Some ran their hands against the fuselage, just to make sure it was real.

A few minutes later Captain Paul and Lt. Turner came walked out wearing black spacesuits. One trainee hastily climbed off the fighter. Captain Paul walked up to Teddy. "Once we turn on the stealth mode, have your section open the doors. I will notify you on your arm band when we are through, and then you can close them again."

"How about when you return," Teddy asked.

"We will land in the back," Captain Paul said. "We won't turn off stealth mode so there will be no need to come back into the hangar." He and Lt. Turner climbed up the access steps that slid out of the side of the fighter and climbed into the access port, which they then closed. A minute later the craft silently rose about ten feet and then shimmered and disappeared. Teddy's section opened the hangar doors and not ten seconds later he received a call on his wrist band to close the doors. The trainees looking out the door could not see where the craft had gone.

When the hangar door was closed, Teddy turned to the trainees. "Okay folks, let's go to the classroom and learn how to fly this thing so we are the next ones who take it out for a spin."

# CHAPTER TWENTY-SEVEN

As the trainees watched, Paul and Liam climbed into the fighter and sealed the hatch. They settled into their seats, or saddles, as Liam now called them, and fastened the straps across their legs and chest. "I'll take her out," Paul said as he brought the systems on-line and lifted the craft up ten feet. "Activate stealth mode," he instructed Al and watched as Section One opened the hangar doors. Paul took the fighter out of the hangar and across the tarmac, until he was hovering twenty feet off the ground halfway down the old runway.

"Configure your side of the console in whatever manner you find most comfortable," Paul instructed.

Liam moved some of the displays around on the virtual board until he had it set in a familiar pattern. He ran navigation on top with stealth and life support over to the side. He set up sensors next to navigation and placed armament below navigation. He glanced questionably over at Paul when he configured armament.

"No, that's fine," Paul said. "We are in a fighter. You should always check armament. Especially with the luck you and I have had on our flights," he added with a chuckle.

Liam noticed that the pulse cannons and phased aray were both in the green and they had a full load of darts. They were not carrying the two heavy ship killer missiles, but otherwise they were fully armed. "Do these always run armed?" Liam asked.

"Yes, except for the missiles. Those are only loaded if the mission calls for them," Paul explained.

Liam checked the modules one more time and then looked at Paul. "I'm as ready as I will ever be," he said. "What is the mission?"

"Call up flight plan Delta," Paul said. "It will take you into a high orbit. Once there I have pre-programed a Nav pattern for you to follow so you can adjust the inertial dampeners to your satisfaction. After that, we will play it by ear."

Liam called up the flight plan and saw it load on the navigation module. "You do want me to fly it, rather than Al, correct?" he asked.

"Of course," Paul said. "You have the controls."

"I have the controls," Liam responded. He

smiled as he took a deep breath and squeezed with his calves. The fighter moved across the runway, slowly gaining speed. Squeezing harder, he dropped his heels and lifted his toes. The fighter angled upwards and increased speed. Liam moved one leg back and the fighter leapt away from the ground, rushing for the sky.

"Avoid the cloud," Paul said conversationally. "You will give away your position by punching a hole through it at this speed."

Liam moved his leg and the fighter dodged the cloud as it continued to climb at a steep angle. The inertial dampeners were on full so there was no sense of motion inside the cockpit. Only the visual displays and the console readouts gave any indication of their movement. The blue sky darkened and turned to black as they left the Earth's atmosphere behind.

The sensor module displayed all the trash circling in space along his flight path as well as the various satellites. The space station's orbit was on the other side of the Earth right now so he did not have to watch for it. Liam checked the shields to ensure that any minor impacts would not be a problem, although at these speeds, minor was a relative term. When he reached high orbit, he keyed in the next program. It displayed several turns, twists and changes in velocity, ending with a full stop. Again, full stop was relative since everything in space was moving.

"This pattern," Liam said, pointing to the course laid out on the nav screen, "is like a dressage test in space."

Paul smiled. "Exactly. You will do it several times. The first time with the inertial dampeners on full, like they are now. Then repeat, each time dialing down the dampeners so there is more force transmitted to the cockpit. You need to determine what amount of force provides you the best feedback. This is the one thing we can't do in VR. And Al will make sure you don't dial it down too much and squish us like bugs."

"Thank you, Al," Liam said.

"My pleasure," Al replied.

Liam ran through the course the first time effortlessly. After the VR fox hunt, this was a cake walk. He repeated it several times while adjusting the dampeners. "How far down do you want me to take them?" he asked after the fourth run.

"You were pulling 3 g's at that last setting. Four to six g's can cause black-out. We are not wearing G-suits, so I rather not do that," Paul said.

"Yea, I'm good with that," Liam said. "Let the fighter pilots brag about how many g's they pulled. I'm a helicopter pilot."

"An F-16 can pull 9 g's, "Paul said. "You pulled 68 g's on that last run. Of course, it wasn't transmitted to the cockpit."

Liam ran the course two more times, adjusting

the dampeners as he flew until he found a comfortable setting. It provided him enough external stimuli so he did not have to look at the console to know how the fighter was moving. He saved that setting as a pre-set for future use.

"You ready for a real test drive," Paul asked.

"Ready as I will ever be," Liam responded.

"Then take us to the Moon."

"The Moon?"

"Yes. Take us to the escape pod. And don't take all day getting there."

Liam smiled. "Right, boss." He pulled up the coordinates for the downed escape pod and had Al configure the optimal flight path. He leaned forward slightly, pushed one leg back and squeezed, clicking his tongue quietly. The fighter leaped forward, with just a slight pressure on the occupants. When he achieved near maximum velocity, he leaned back in a neutral position, but not enough to activate deceleration. Liam had to keep reminding himself that in space you did not need constant thrust to maintain your speed. The correlation between thrust, speed and acceleration took on a totally different function in space than on Earth.

In twenty minutes, he was crossing over to the dark side of the moon. As they neared the crash site, Liam looked over to Paul. "Do you want to take her in or should I?" he asked, remembering the last time they were there.

"Oh, you do it," Paul said. "You are the pilot."

Liam took them down and hovered twenty feet above the crashed escape pod. His foot prints were clearly visible in the lunar dirt since there wasn't any wind to blow them away. It had only been about six months ago that he had walked on the Moon. Now he was flying a space fighter. His whole world had changed that night. Liam wondered what the next six months held for him and whether he would still be as delighted to be flying in space.

"You've come a long way," Paul said, probably sensing his thoughts.

"You did promise me an adventure of a lifetime," Liam said.

"I did," Paul agreed. "Let's hope it works out," he added somberly.

"I will always thank you for bringing me in," Liam responded seriously. "Whatever happens, I would rather be up here fighting, than down there unaware. Or worse, helpless."

They both stared at the crashed escape pod. Paul broke the silence. "Okay, here is the next step." He loaded a course that took them a couple hundred miles across the moon's surface. "Follow this course," he instructed.

"That doesn't look that hard," Liam said as he studied the course.

"We'll see," Paul said. "Keep a constant 100 feet above the actual surface of the Moon. That means if you are traveling over a large crater, you follow the contours of the crater. Don't just shoot across."

"How fast?" Liam asked.

"As fast as you can," Paul said. "I would suggest you start slow and then speed up. Try not to pancake us against the side of a crater."

"Yes, Sir," Liam said. He adjusted the Nav screen to provide a heads-up display of his course along with markers indicating height changes. When he finished, the display showed him a virtual tunnel, rather than just a line to his destination. He started slowly and then quickly sped up. The display remained green initially, even after he dropped into the first large crater. There was a quick flash of red as he crested the crater's rim and did not drop down fast enough, but at 100 mph, he thought that was okay.

He increased his speed to 150 mph and then 200 mph. The red flashes increased, but remained momentary as he adjusted his course. When he finished the course, he brought the fighter to a stop, hovering a hundred feet above the lunar surface. Paul pulled up an overview of their flight. There were a lot of red marks where he came out of the nav tunnel, but none lasted very long.

Paul did not comment on the red marks. Rather he said, "Obviously, in a real setting you would have Al fly this course as he can do it much faster and with fewer errors."

Liam was trying to figure out if that was criticism when Paul continued. "Now go back to the starting point. This time set your course for twenty-five feet and keep your speed over 200 mph. And don't hurt the paint job."

"Twenty-five feet? Are you kidding?"

"No. This is a fighter. Fly it like one."

"I don't think fighters fly this close to the ground," Liam said.

"Sure, they do," Paul said. "When no one is watching. And don't give me that helicopter excuse. When I was in the Army, the senior warrant officers would fly nap-of-the-Earth. We flew below tree-top level. I have had tree limbs hit my feet when I was sitting in the door gunner seat and have flown under bridges. And they did that at speed. This is a fighter. Fly it like one."

"Okay," Liam said, none too sure as he adjusted the Nav display. "Al, keep me above fifteen feet," he instructed.

"Al, disregard," Paul countered. "Turn off safeties."

"Your funeral," Al said as warning lights appeared on the console showing that safeties had been turned off.

"Are you sure?" Liam said.

"You have to learn it some time," Paul said as he leaned back in his seat, arms crossed.

Liam checked his settings two more times before starting back at twenty feet. He increased his speed as he gained confidence. At 100 mph he was sweating under his spacesuit.

"Relax," Paul said. "You can do this."

Another red spot flashed as Liam went too low and he overcompensated by shooting too high before coming back into the green.

"You need to flow with this," Paul said. "Don't fight it. Use the force, as you love to say."

"I... don't... have... the... damn... force," Liam said through clenched teeth as another red flash lit the Nav screen.

"Sure, you do," Paul said. He leaned forward. "Override," he said as he boosted the fighter. Suddenly they were flying at 250 mph.

"What the hell," Liam yelled as the fighter shot forward, red lights flashing as he flew too high over a crater.

"Twenty feet, keep her at twenty," Paul said.

Liam fought the controls as the fighter went from fifty feet to ten feet. A large crater approached quickly. Liam had to bring the fighter up to get over the lip and then drop fast into the bowl and then up the other side, before bringing it back down. The Nav screen was red with only an occasional green now.

"Twenty feet, twenty feet," Paul was saying it like a mantra.

Liam didn't know how much farther he had to fly, he was fixated on what was immediately in front of him and trying to keep his craft in the thin green tunnel displayed on his screen. Another crater wall came up and he leaped over it, trying to come down into the bowl like the last two. As he crested this crater, he realized it was much smaller. He jerked his feet up and the fighter shot straight up out of the crater. Realizing his error, he pushed back down, and caught the craft within five feet of the ground. Another crater ridge. He jumped it and pushed down to go into the bowl, only to find there was a crater within a crater.

The fighter slammed into the second crater wall hard. He was thrown forward against his restraints as the fighter blasted through the crater wall in a fountain of dirt and shot into the air.

"I have the controls," Paul said as he brought the fighter to a stop and then looped back to where they had impacted. Lunar dirt was slowly raining down in the Moon's one-sixth gravity.

"Whoa, what a ride," Paul said, laughing.

"Are you insane?" Liam shouted. "Why did you goose it? We could have been killed."

"It's like the VR program, you have to push it to learn," Paul answered.

"Yes, but the VR program is not real. You get another life. Out here you do not. Dead is dead," Liam said, getting mad.

"I'm sorry," Paul said. "But I needed to know what you would do. If you are going to be my pilot, I need to know that you can cut it."

"To see if I got you killed?" Liam said.

"No. To see if you would even try to keep it at twenty feet or if you would just quit. And, of course, to see if you could do it," Paul said. "And you did. You stuck to it."

"I crashed through a crater wall at 250 mph," Liam shouted. "I honestly don't know why we are still alive."

"We crashed through it with full shields on," Paul explained. "And I had Al make sure we did not hit anything too hard."

"You told Al to turn all safeties off," Liam objected.

"This is my ship," Paul said. "It has a lot of subroutines. We didn't turn them all off."

Liam sat there trying to control his emotions. He had been scared to death and now he was madder than hell. He took several deep breaths. On the screen the dust from his impact with the crater wall was almost settled. "You said you would warn me about anything scary."

"What?"

"When I met Sally the first time," Liam explained. "You said you would tell me when something was going to be scary. That was scary."

"I couldn't warn you and conduct the test," Paul said.

"Are there any more tests like that?" Liam asked.

"No. That was the last one. And if it makes you feel any better, you passed," Paul said.

"I'm not sure," Liam said. "Ask me tomorrow."

"Fair enough," Paul said. "Now, take her home. You have the controls."

"I have the controls," Liam acknowledged. He had Al plot the course, and then he turned the fighter and started following the navigation markers. Al had plotted a course that took them several miles off the surface of the Moon before they came out from the dark side. Liam followed the course, slowly increasing the fighter's speed.

"An adventure of a lifetime," Liam said after a few moments.

"Yep, an adventure of a lifetime," Paul agreed.

"Oh, what the hell," Liam chuckled. He goosed the fighter and left the flight path, dropping down to level off fifty feet over the Moon's surface. He punched it again and crossed the terminator line into the sunlight at over 2,000 mph, before pulling away from the Moon and accelerating to his projected flight path.

# CHAPTER TWENTY-EIGHT

As Liam headed for Earth, he leaned forward and pushed it. Monitoring the consoles seemed second nature after VR as he balanced the power requirements of the engines and shields, while watching the sensors for any foreign objects. A strike by even a small object at these speeds would be cataclysmic. Meanwhile, Al kept recalculating their route to show when and how much Liam would have to decelerate to safely enter Earth's atmosphere and the power requirements to do so.

Once again Liam was amazed by the beauty of Earth from space. The blue, green and brown marble, covered with cotton candy whisps of white clouds, contrasted sharply with the black of space surrounding it. It was easy to forget all of your problems while staring at the Earth. But the fact that he was in a fighter and might have to protect his world gnawed in the back of his mind.

Liam did not cut his speed until Al's calculations showed that he would have to do one complete deceleration orbit around Earth before he could safely reenter its atmosphere. Liam came in high and fast as he leaned back to decelerate. He stayed above all Earth's satellites and assorted space junk as he decelerated.

"Plot your course so it ends near the space station," Paul suggested. "I always do a flyby there."

"Do you ever think of turning off stealth?" Liam asked

"Oh, worse. I've fantasized about doing a spacewalk and knocking on their airlock," Paul said with a laugh. "Can you imagine their reaction?"

Liam laughed. "That would be a good one. Excuse me, do you have any Grey Poupon? We have run out."

They were both laughing, trying to imagine the looks on the astronauts faces, when the sensor module beeped.

"What is that?" Liam said as an icon showed up in the heads-up display.

Paul looked at the display for a second before crying out, "I've got the controls, shields full, weapons hot!" He spun the fighter around and accelerated backwards, with the front of the fighter facing the approaching object. He opened fire with the light cannons. Twin lines of cohesive light, like tracers, shot out from the fighter, tracking towards the object. They intersected and a bright white light exploded and then quickly dissipated into nothing.

"Full sweep, active scan," Paul commanded as he slowed the fighter.

"What was that?" Liam asked as the scan came back negative. The whole event had lasted five seconds.

"That," Paul said as he conducted a second sensor sweep, "was another one of those contact mines. Why is it," he continued, "that every time I come up here with you, we get attacked? It never happens with anyone else."

"Just lucky, I guess," Liam answered, taken aback by how fast things had gone from fun and games to almost fatal.

"Next time I'll let you keep the controls," Paul said. "But you haven't been checked out on weapons yet."

"That's okay," Liam said. "I don't mind."

"Okay," Paul said. "Take the controls and take us home."

"I have the controls," Liam said.

"You have the controls," Paul confirmed.

Liam set a course for the base and headed into the atmosphere. "I suspect someone saw that," Liam said.

"Hard not to notice that explosion," Paul agreed. "But that is not our problem. We will let them try to figure it out." Paul called Teddy on the wrist band and told him to open the hangar doors. "Since things are starting to heat up, I want to keep a fighter with us on standby," Paul explained his change in plans to Liam. "That way we don't have to wait for one to be ferried over from the Pacific."

Liam thought that was a good idea. He guided the fighter into the dark hangar and the doors closed behind them. Paul activated the internal hangar lights as Liam turned off the stealth mode, spun the craft around and brought it down on its four landing skids, before powering it down. All the trainees had come into the hangar and were standing by the side as Paul and Liam climbed out of the top hatch and down off the fighter. It was 1930 hours.

"Everyone to the classroom," Paul called to the assembled trainees as he led the way, along with Lt. Turner, both still wearing their spacesuits, but with the helmets retracted. They all filed into the classroom and Paul and Liam went to the front. The trainees filled the rest of the room.

"I forgot that we moved your chairs," Paul said. "So, sit on your saddles, but don't put on your VR." When the trainees had taken their seats, or saddles, Paul continued. "We just had a reminder about how serious our training is. As we were coming back from a routine training flight, we came across a Red Force contact mine. These mines have a seek and destroy function. I don't know what it is about Lt. Turner, but this is the second time that we have been targeted by one of these. Let me show you what they do."

He turned to the screen behind him. "Al, play the contact clip." The screen lit up showing the displays, but not the pilots. There was no sound. "We were joking about knocking on the door of the space station and watching their reaction when this happened," Paul said. An icon appeared on the heads-up display. A second later the fighter spun around and accelerated backwards, while twin lines of coherent light shot out from the fighter, tracking towards the object. The object exploded and then quickly dissipated into nothing.

"I will play it again, since it went so fast," Paul said as the scene repeated itself. "Five seconds," Paul said. "The whole incident lasted five seconds. I'm sure your previous flight instructors stressed how quickly things can go sideways. Here is a perfect example. That mine can destroy a fighter. So just remember. Training may be fun and games, but the end result of what we are doing is deadly serious. One mistake, one moment of inattention, and it could be your last." Captain Paul looked out at the assembled trainees. "Now if you have left any food here, I'm going to get something to eat before heading home." With that he strode off the stage into the breakroom, leaving Lt. Turner and the trainees in the classroom. It happened so fast, Liam did not get a chance to call everyone to attention.

When Captain Paul left, the trainees clustered around Liam to hear the details of the story. One thing was certain, things were about to change.

# EPILOGUE

"RED ALERT, RED ALERT. THIS IS NOT A DRILL. THIS IS NOT A DRILL. RED FORCE CAPITOL SHIP IN VICINITY. DEFENSE PLAN BRAVO-9."

Lt. Liam Turner ran down the corridor to the launch pad where his fighter was parked. In the one-sixth lunar gravity, he bounded, making good time to the locker room where his spacesuit was hanging. Other members of Hunter Squadron ran in and put on their suits before heading through the airlock to their fighters.

Liam moved in slow motion as he tried to control his breathing. He had been training for this moment for months, ever since the Delorians had warned that a large armada was amassing outside the Jupiter jump gate, waiting to invade the Sol system and attack Earth. The Delorians would fight the attackers at the Jupiter gate while the humans would defend Earth from their base on the Moon if the attackers got past the Delorians.

That was the plan, Liam told himself. That is why they had been training for the past several months, why Captain Paul had established Lunar Patrol, and why Liam had been pulled out of flight school in Pensacola to learn to fly Delorian fighters. They were ready.

But they weren't ready. As XO of Hunter Squadron Liam was privy to the overview. In every drill, in every computer simulation, Lunar Patrol lost. As sophisticated as the Delorian fighters were, if Red Force got past the Delorians, Lunar Patrol was wiped out every time. A group of fighters could not defeat a Red Force capital ship. There just was not enough fire power.

Liam pulled at his spacesuit. Why couldn't he get it on? Other members of Hunter Squadron had come in, donned their suits and left. Why couldn't he? An alarm sounded as he struggled to put on his suit. They were losing air pressure. He had seconds to get his suit on or he would die. His hands grouped at his suit. It snagged at his knees and elbows. It wouldn't seal. The alarm rose and fell. He was already having trouble breathing as he pulled the suit across his chest. Now the helmet. He pulled it over his head and sealed it. Still not enough air. He was suffocating in his suit. Groping for his helmet seal, he tried to pull it back off, but it was stuck. He could not breath...

Liam awoke with a start, his blanket over his

head. Gasping for breath, he realized he was lying on his cot, soaked in sweat. He glanced at his wrist. 0300 hours. He quietly stood up. Around him in the bunk room, the other members of Hunter Squadron slept. Trying to shake the remnants of his nightmare, he walked out of the bunk room into the open bay of the deserted World War II hanger.

He walked over to the Delorian fighter that was the sole occupant of the vast hanger and ran his hand across its sleek fuselage.

"Would you like to enter the fighter," a voice spoke in his head.

"No, thank you Al," Liam subvocalized. "Just going for a walk."

"The perimeter is clear," Al responded. "Temperature is sixty-seven degrees and the moon is three-quarters. Plenty of ambient light."

"Another nice night on the Gulf Coast," Liam said as he headed for the hanger door. Being based in the Florida Panhandle did have its benefits. Liam walked outside and headed across the old, deserted runway. He looked up at the stars. Strange he thought. Barely six months ago he just saw stars. He paid little attention to speculation about life on other planets or the odd story about UFOs. That was before. Before Paul had recruited him on a mission to rescue an alien who had crashed on the Moon. Before he had learned that aliens had been living on Earth for centuries. Before he had been invited into the select few humans who interacted with these aliens. Before he knew that an alien armada was about to attack Earth.

No wonder he was having nightmares. He almost envied the rest of humanity, who still had no idea about aliens or the impending attack. Well, they were about to have a rude awakening, Liam thought.

Walking slowly across the warm asphalt of the deserted runway, Liam could not imagine being ready when the attack came. He still couldn't fly the Delorian fighter, let alone fight it. Well, that was Paul's worry. He wondered how Paul slept at night.

Liam took another glance at the night sky. The three-quarter Moon had cleared the trees and was slowly climbing up the night sky. Somewhere on that Moon the Delorians were building their new base. Liam had walked on the Moon once. What would it be like to live on the Moon? He was about to find out. One thing was certain, Paul had delivered on his promise to give Liam the adventure of a lifetime.

# AFTERWORD

Read, *Lunar Patrol - Defending Earth*, for the exciting conclusion of this series.

# ABOUT THE AUTHOR

## David Hiers

David Hiers has had many adventures as a lifeguard, firefighter, Army Captain and as a lawyer. He currently lives on a horse farm outside Pensacola, Florida with his beautiful wife and daughter, an overactive imagination, and too many critters.

# BOOKS IN THIS SERIES

## LUNAR PATROL SERIES

**Lunar Patrol - Hunter Squadron**

**Lunar Patrol - Defending Earth**

# BOOKS BY THIS AUTHOR

**First Contact**

**First Contact - Return**

**First Contact - Cube**

**Lunar Patrol - Hunter Squadron**

**Lunar Patrol - Defending Earth**